LONGMAN IMPRINT BOOKS

# Twelve War Stories

selected and edited by
**John L. Foster**
*Head of Lower School*
*Lord Williams's School, Thame*

**Longman**

LONGMAN GROUP LIMITED
*Longman House*
*Burnt Mill, Harlow, Essex,*

First published 1980
Second impression 1982

ISBN 0 582 23019 5

Set in 10/11pt. Baskerville 169

Printed in Hong Kong by
Yu Luen Offset Printing Factory Limited

# Contents

|                                              | Page |
|----------------------------------------------|------|
| Editor's Note                                | vi   |
|                                              |      |
| Richard Aldington    **At All Costs**        | 1    |
| H. E. Bates    **It's Just the Way It Is**   | 19   |
| Ambrose Bierce    **A Horseman in the Sky**  | 25   |
| Ray Bradbury    **The Drummer Boy of Shiloh**| 33   |
| Charles Causley    **Looking for Annie**     | 39   |
| Stephen Crane    **A Mystery of Heroism**    | 49   |
| Roald Dahl    **Beware of the Dog**          | 55   |
| William Faulkner    **Shall Not Perish**     | 67   |
| Robert Graves    **Christmas Truce**         | 79   |
| Ian Hay    **The Non-Combatant**             | 97   |
| James S. Kenary    **Going Home**            | 119  |
| Alun Lewis    **The Raid**                   | 135  |
|                                              |      |
| Questions for Discussion and Suggestions for Writing | 144 |
| The Authors                                  | 149  |
| Further Reading                              | 154  |
| Films                                        | 157  |
| Acknowledgements                             | 161  |

# Editor's Note

The aim of this collection is to provide student readers with a range of stories that give insights into the experience of war from the point of view of those who are involved as combatants. While most of the stories deal with the experiences of soldiers, two of the stories are about airmen and one is a naval story. The object is to present the student reader with stories of quality, which give a realistic picture of what it feels like to be involved as a participant in an armed conflict, and thus to counterbalance the false pictures of warfare that are often presented on the screen and in war comics.

J.L.F.

# At All Costs

# At All Costs

**Richard Aldington**

*First World War*


"Blast!"

Captain Hanley, commanding "B" Company, stumbled over a broken duckboard and fell forward against the side of the trench. His tilted helmet shielded his face, but the trench wall felt oozy and soggy to his naked hand as he tried to steady himself.

"Mind that hole, Parker."

"Very good, sir."

He felt wet mud soaking through his breeches above the short gum boots, and his right sleeve was wet to the elbow. He fumbled in his gas bag, also wet with slimy mud, to see that the mask goggles were unbroken. OK, but he swore again with a sort of exasperated groan over the crashing bruise on his right knee.

"Are you 'it, sir?"

"No, I only fell in that mucking hole again. I've told the ser'ant-major umpteen times to get it mended. One of these days the brigadier'll fall into it and then there'll be hell to pay. Help me find my torch. I hope the bloody thing isn't broken."

The two men groped in the darkness, fingering the slimy mud and tilted broken duckboards. Suddenly they crashed helmets.

"Sorry, sir."

"All right, sorry."

"Doesn't seem to be 'ere, sir."

"Never mind, we'll look for it in the morning."

They stumbled on cautiously. The trench was very deep (old German communication), very dark, very shell-smashed, very muddy. A black, heavy-clouded night, about an hour before dawn. Occasionally a strange ghostly glow appeared as a distant Very light[1] was fired, and made for them a near dark horizon of tumbled shell-tormented parapet. The trench swerved, and Hanley dimly made out the shape of three crosses – Canadians. Halfway. Fifty yards farther on was another turn, where a piece of corrugated iron revetment[2] had been flung on to the top of

[1] a light sent up to illuminate the enemy's position or to give a signal at night
[2] supporting wall

the high parapet, where its jagged outline looked like a grotesque heraldic dragon.

It had been an ideal night for gas and would be an ideal dawn – heavy, windless, foggy – for a surprise attack. Hanley had been up and about the trenches most of the night. Since that rotten gas attack on the Somme, where he lost twenty-three men, he took no risks. Up and down the trenches, warning the NCOs[1] to look out for gas. Now he was on the way to his advance posts. Be there in case of an attack...

Splash, squelch, splodge. Somebody coming towards them.

"Who are you?"

"Mockery."

"Is that the word tonight, Parker?"

"Yessir."

"That you, Hanley?" Voice coming towards them.

"Hullo, Williams. I thought you were in Hurdle Alley?"

"I was, but I thought I'd have a look at these posts. They're a hell of a way from the front line."

"I know. Damn this organisation in depth. Are they all right?"

"Yes. He sent over about forty minnies,[2] Ser'ant Cramp said, but no casualties. He was flipping over some of those flying pineapples[3] when I left."

From their own back areas came an irregular but ceaseless crashing of artillery. Heavy shells shrilled high above them as they swooped at enemy communications and night parties.

"Strafing[4] the old Boche[5] a good bit tonight," said Williams.

"Yes, it's been quite heavy. Might almost be a windup at HQ."

"Boche are very quiet tonight."

"Yes; well, cheerio. Tell Thompson to keep our breakfast hot; and don't stand down until I get back."

"Right you are, cheerio."

Hanley visited his posts. They were established in a ruined and unrepaired German trench at the foot of a long forward slope. This had once been the British front line, but was now held only by scattered observation posts, with the main front line several

---

[1] non-commissioned officers
[2] bombs, from the German *Mine*, mine
[3] German mortar bombs, with wind vanes
[4] heavily bombarding
[5] Germans

hundred yards to the rear. The British bombardment increased, and the shrill scream of the passing shells was almost continuous. Very lights and rockets went up from the German lines. Hanley cursed the loss of his torch – damned difficult to get about without it. He came to the first post.

"You there, Ser'ant Tomlinson?"

A figure moved in the darkness.

"Yes, sir."

"Anything to report?"

"No, sir."

"Mr Williams said there were some minnies and pineapples."

"Yes, sir, but it's very quiet, sir."

"Um. Any patrols still out?"

"No, sir, all in."

"Very well. Carry on, ser'ant."

"Very good, sir."

Much the same news at the other posts. Hanley returned to Number 1 post, nearest the communication trench, at dawn. The men were standing to.[1] Hanley got on the fire-step in a shell-smashed abandoned bay, and watched with his glasses slung round his neck. The artillery had died down to a couple of batteries, when the first perceptible lightening of the air came. Hanley felt cold in his mud-soaked breeches and tunic. Very gradually, very slowly, the darkness dissipated, as if thin imperceptible veils were being rolled up in a transformation scene. The British wire became visible. In the trembling misty light No Man's Land[2] seemed alive with strange shapes and movements. Hanley pressed cold hands on his hot eyes, puffy with lack of sleep. He looked again. Yes, yes, surely, they were climbing over the parapet and lying down in front. He seized a rifle leaning against the trench, loaded with an SOS rocket bomb. Funny Sergeant Tomlinson and the men were so silent. Perhaps he was imagining things, the same old dawn-mirage movement which had been responsible for so many false alarms. He waited a couple of minutes with closed eyes, and then looked very carefully through his glasses. Silly ass! The men coming over the parapets were the German wire pickets. He put the rifle down, glad the men had not seen him, and went round the traverse[3] to Sergeant Tomlinson and Parker.

---

[1] standing with firearms at the ready
[2] the area between the British front-line trenches and the German trenches
[3] right-angle bend in a trench

"Stand to for another twenty minutes, ser'ant, and then let two men from Number 2 post and two from Number 4 go and get your breakfasts."

"Very good, sir."

On the way back Hanley found his torch – the glass bulb was smashed; like most things in this bloody war, he reflected. Well, they'd passed another dawn without an attack – that was something. He got on a fire-step in the main line and took another look. A cloudy but rainless morning. Not a sign of life in the enemy trenches, scarcely a sound. He gave the order to stand down, and sent Parker to join his section for breakfast.

The company dug-out was a large one, built as the head-quarters of a German battalion. It was remarkably lousy. Hanley threw his torch, revolver-belt, and helmet on his wire and sacking bed, and sat down on a box beside a small table laid with four knives and forks on a newspaper. He felt tired, too tired even to enjoy the hot bacon and eggs which formed the infantry officers' best meal of the day. The three subalterns chatted. Hanley pushed away his plate and stood up.

"I'm going to turn in. Tell the signaller to wake me if anything important happens."

"Right-o."

Hanley hung up his revolver and helmet, arranged his pack as a pillow, swung himself still booted and wet on to the bed, and wrapped himself in a blanket. For a few minutes he lay drowsily, listening to the throb of blood in his head and the quiet mutter of the other officers. His eyes still ached even when shut. He drowsed, then half awoke as he remembered that he had not indented[1] for enough ammunition, decided that could wait, and – was dead asleep.

Hanley opened his eyes and lay quite still. Why were they talking so loudly? In a flash he was wide awake and swung up, sitting with his legs over the side of the bed. The colonel. Damn! Being found asleep like that! And, of course, the colonel would not know that he had been up and down the line all night. Damn! Well, never mind. He gave one dab with both hands at his rumpled hair, and stood up.

"Good morning, sir."

[1] ordered (normally in writing)

"Oh, good morning, Hanley. Williams said you'd been up all night. Sorry to disturb you."

"Quite all right, sir."

A large-scale trench map of their sector was spread on the table, half concealing another smaller-scale artillery map of the whole district.

"Just sit down for a few minutes, Hanley. I've got important news."

The other officers grouped beside them, gazing at the colonel and listening.

"Very important news," the colonel went on in a slow voice, "and not particularly pleasant, I'm afraid."

He pulled a neat bundle of documents from his pocket, opened one labelled "SECRET AND CONFIDENTIAL" and spread it on the table. They all gazed at it – the inexorable decree of Fate – and then again at the colonel, the agent of that Fate, of all their fates.

"That is a confidential document from Corps Headquarters. I'll tell you briefly what it is, and you can look it over afterwards. The night before last the division on our left made an identification raid, and captured a prisoner. From this and other information it seems certain that we shall be attacked – tomorrow morning – about an hour before dawn."

Each of the four company officers drew a short imperceptible breath, glanced at each other and then quickly away. Hanley leaned his elbow on the table.

"Yes, sir?"

"It will be a surprise attack, with a very short but violent preliminary bombardment." The colonel spoke very slowly and deliberately, looking down absently at the map, and gently twisting the lowest button of his tunic with the fingers of his right hand. "All reports confirm our information, and the Air Force report great enemy activity behind the lines. You heard the bombardment of their communications last night."

"Yes, sir."

There was complete silence in the dug-out, as the colonel paused. A pile of tin plates fell with a clatter in the servants' compartment. None of the officers moved. Hanley noticed how clean the colonel's gas bag was.

"There will probably be twenty to thirty German divisions in the attack, which will be on a sixteen-mile front. We are about in the middle."

"Yes, sir."

6

The colonel moved on his box. He stretched out all the fingers of his left hand, and tapped rapidly on the table alternately with the stretched little finger and thumb.

"The Canadian Corps and several reserve divisions are being brought up at once to occupy a position about five miles to our rear. They cannot fully man the whole battle line before three tomorrow afternoon. Our duty is to delay the enemy advance until that time or longer. Our positions must be held at all costs, to the last man."

There was a long silence. The colonel ceased drumming with his fingers and looked at them.

"Have you any questions to ask?"

"Yes, sir. Am I to leave my posts out?"

"Two hours before dawn, you will withdraw them to strengthen your own line. One section, with a sergeant and a subaltern, will remain at the end of the communication trench. The subaltern will be a volunteer. His duty is to fire a green light when the German attacking line reaches him. The artillery barrage will then shorten to defend your line. You, Hanley, will have a Very-light pistol loaded with a red light, and you will fire it when the first German jumps into your trench. The object, of course, is to inform the artillery when they must shorten the defensive barrage."

"Yes, sir."

"Any more questions?"

"No, sir, not for the moment."

"You'll arrange with your officers, Hanley, as to which shall volunteer to fire the green light."

"Very good, sir."

"And I want you to come to a conference of company officers with the brigadier at Battalion Headquarters this afternoon."

"Very good, sir. What time?"

"Oh, make it three o'clock."

"Very well, sir."

The colonel rose.

"You know your battle positions, of course; but we'll discuss that this afternoon. Oh, by the bye, I'm sending up green envelopes for everyone in the company this morning. The letters must be sent down by runner at four. Of course, not a word about the attack must be mentioned either to NCOs or men until after the letters have gone."

"Of course, sir."

"And – er – naturally you will not mention the matter your-selves."

"No, sir, of course not."

"All right. Good-bye. Will you come along with me, Hanley? I should like to walk round your main defence line with you."

"Very good, sir."

There was silence in the dug-out. They could hear the colonel and Hanley scuffling up the low dug-out stairs. Williams tapped a cigarette on his case and bent down to light it at the candle burning on the table. He puffed a mouthful of smoke, with a twist to his lips.

"Well, that's that. Napoo,[1] eh?"

"Looks like it."

"What about a drink?"

"Right-o."

Williams shouted:

"Thomp-sooon."

From the distance came a muffled: "Sir?"

A Tommy[2] appeared in the doorway.

"Bring us a bottle of whisky and the mugs."

"Very good, sir."

All that day Hanley was in a state of dazed hebetude[3], from which he emerged from time to time. He felt vaguely surprised that everything was so much as usual. There were sentries at their posts, runners going along the trenches, an occasional airplane overhead, a little artillery – just the ordinary routine of trench warfare. And yet within twenty-four hours their trenches would be obliterated, he and thousands with him would be dead, obliterated, unless by some chance, some odd freak, he was made prisoner. He heard repeated over and over again in his head the words: "Position must be held at all costs, position must be held at all costs." He felt suddenly angry. Held at all costs! All jolly fine and large to write from the safety of Montreuil, but what about those who had to make good such dramatic sentiments with their lives? The front was ridiculously denuded of men – why, his own under-strength company held very nearly a

[1] Army slang – "There is nothing to be done", from the French "Il n'y en a plus"
[2] private in the British Army
[3] a state of being dull or drowsy

battalion front, and had a flank to guard as well. If they fought like madmen and stood to the last man, they might hold up three waves – an hour at most. And they were asked to hold out for nearly twelve hours! Ridiculous, good God, ridiculous!

He found the colonel shaking him by the arm.

"What's the matter with you, Hanley? You don't seem to hear what I'm saying."

"I beg your pardon, sir. I . . . "

"I think you ought to bring a Lewis gun up to this point. You've got an excellent field of fire here."

"Very good, sir."

Hanley noted the change to be made in his field service message book. They walked on, and the colonel made various other suggestions – so many orders – which Hanley duly noted. The colonel paused at the corner of the communication trench leading to Battalion Headquarters. He waved to the orderlies to stand apart.

"We'll discuss the general plan of defence at the conference this afternoon. Make a note of anything that occurs to you, any information you want, and bring it up."

"Right, sir."

The colonel hesitated a moment.

"It's a very difficult position, Hanley, I know, but we must all do our duty."

"Of course, sir."

"I shall lead the counter-attack of the Reserve Company myself."

"Yes, sir."

"A great deal depends on our putting up a good show."

"Yes, sir."

"I suggest you go round to the dug-out and speak to all your men this evening. Put a good face on it, you know. Tell them we are all prepared, and shall easily beat off the attack, and that reinforcements are being hurried up to relieve us. And above all impress upon them that these trenches *must* be held at all costs."

"Very good, sir."

The colonel held out his hand.

"I may not have another opportunity to speak to you in private. Goodbye, and the best of luck. I know you'll do your duty."

"Thank you, sir. Goodbye."

"Goodbye."

When Hanley stooped under the low entrance of the dug-out chamber, the three subalterns were seated round the table with flushed cheeks, talking loudly. The whisky bottle was more than half-empty. A sudden spurt of anger shot through him. He strode up to the table and knocked the cork level with the top of the bottle neck with one hard smack of his hand. He spoke harshly:

"What's this nonsense?"

Williams, the eldest of the three subalterns, answered, half-defiantly, half-ashamedly:

"We're only having a drink. Where's the harm?"

"Only a drink! Before lunch! Now, look here, you fellows. The whisky that's left in that bottle is all that's going to be drunk in this mess between now and dawn tomorrow. Understand? One of the damned stupidities of this damned war is that every officer thinks it's the thing to be a boozer. It isn't. The men don't drink. They get a tablespoon of rum a day. Why should we make sots of ourselves? We're responsible for their lives. See? And we're responsible for these trenches. We've got to leave 'em on stretchers or stay here and manure 'em. See? We've got a bloody rotten job ahead of us, a stinking rotten job, and I wish those who ordered it were here to carry out their own damned orders. But they're not. Not bloody likely. But the people at home trust us. We're responsible to them, first and foremost. We took on the job, and we've got to carry it out. And carry it out dead bloody sober. Got me?"

The men were silent, looking sheepishly at the newspaper on the table with its wet rings from mug bottoms. Hanley took an empty mug and tossed some of the whisky from Williams's mug into it.

"Drink up. Here's hell!"

They drank.

Hanley shouted:

"Thomp-soooon!"

Thompson appeared in the door.

"Take those mugs away."

"Very good, sir."

"How many bottles of whisky have you?"

"Three, sir."

"Bring them here, and a sandbag."

"Very good, sir."

Hanley scribbled a few words in his message book, and tore out the slip. He put the bottles in the sandbag.

"Parker!"

Parker in his turn appeared.

"Sir?"

"Take that sandbag down to Battalion HQ. Give it to one of the officers, and bring back his signed receipt."

"Very good, sir."

The other officers exchanged glances. Williams, who had his back turned to Hanley, made a grimace of derision. The others frowned at him.

Hanley was busy throughout the day, making arrangements, giving orders, attending the conference – which lasted a long time – and going round to speak to the men. He only had time to write a very brief letter to his wife, enclosing one still briefer for his father. He wrote calmly, almost coldly in his effort to avoid emotion and self-pity. He even managed to squeeze out a joke for each letter. As soon as they were finished the two letters vanished in the open sandbag containing the company mail, and the runner started at once for Headquarters. Somehow it was a relief to have those letters gone. The last links with England, with life, were broken. Finished, done with, almost forgotten. It was easier to carry on now.

But was it? There was that damned business of the volunteer subaltern. Hanley rubbed his clenched fist against his cheek, and found that he had forgotten to shave. He called his servant and told him to bring some hot water in a cigarette tin. Shaving for the last time. Hardly worth it, really. Still, must be done. Morale, and all that.

He shaved carefully. One of the subalterns went out to relieve the officer on duty. One was asleep. Williams was writing a situation report. Hanley bit the back of his hand hard, then shoved both hands in his breeches pockets, looking at Williams' bent head.

"Williams!"

Williams looked up.

"Yes?"

"There's this business of the volunteer to –"

"Oh, that's all settled."

"Settled!"

"Yes. I'm going."

"You're going! But you've only been married two months."

"Yes. That's why I thought I'd like to get it over as quickly as possible."

"But I was going to put your platoon at the end of Hurdle Alley. You might just be able to get back to battalion, you know."

"And feel a swine for the rest of my life – which would be about two hours? Thanks. No, I'd rather get it over, if you don't mind, Hanley."

"Oh, all right."

They were silent. Then Hanley said:

"Well, I'll just go and talk to the men ... er ... So long."

"So long."

All working parties were cancelled to give the men as much rest as possible, but there was inevitably a lot of extra work, bringing up ammunition, rations, and water. As soon as dusk fell the whole Reserve Company and some pioneers came up to strengthen the wire. The British artillery was ceaselessly active. Hardly a shot came from the German line – an ominous sign.

After dinner Hanley lay down to sleep for a few hours. Must be as fresh as possible. He wrapped the blanket up to his chin and shut his eyes. The other three off duty were lying down, too. But Hanley could not sleep. It was all so strange, so strange, and yet so ordinary. Just like any other night, and yet the last night. Inevitably the last night? How could they escape, with orders to hold on at all costs? Half of them would go in the bombardment, which would be terrific. Bombs, bullets, and bayonets would finish off the rest. The dug-outs would be wrecked with bombs and high explosive charges. A few of the wounded might be picked up later. A few of the men might escape down Hurdle Alley after the officers were gone. But no, the NCOs could be relied on to hold out to the last. They were done for, napoo. No *après la guerre* for *them – bon soir*, toodle-oo, good-byeeee. The silly words repeated and repeated in his brain until he hated them. He opened his eyes and gazed at the familiar dug-out. His wire bed was at an angle to the others, and he could see the shapes of Williams and the two other officers muffled up silent in their blankets – as still and silent as they would be in twenty-four hours' time. There was the candle burning in the holder roughly bent from a tin biscuit box. The flame was absolutely steady in the airless, earthy smelling dug-out. There were the boxes for seats, the table with its maps, tins of cigarettes, chits, and the five mugs beside the whisky bottle for the last parting drink. The bare, murky walls of chalk were damp and clammy-looking with condensed breath. The revolvers, helmets, and gas bags were hung at the bed-heads. He listened to the other men breathing, and felt an absurd regret at leaving the dug-out to be smashed. After all, that and other dug-outs like it were the only home they had known for months and months. Breaking up the happy home! He became aware that he felt a bit sickish, that he had been feeling like that for several hours, and pretending not to.

He gently drew his wrist from under the blanket and looked at his luminous watch. Eleven thirty-five. He had to be up at two – must get some sleep. With almost a start he noticed that Williams was looking at his own watch in the same stealthy way. So he couldn't sleep either. Poor devil. Profoundly, almost insanely in love with that wife of his. Poor devil. But still, for the matter of that, so was Hanley in love with his wife. His heart seemed to turn in his body, and he felt an acute pain in the muscles above it as he suddenly realized fully that it was all over, that he would never see her again, never feel her mouth pressed to his, never again touch her lovely, friendly body. He clutched his hand over his face until it hurt to prevent himself from groaning. God, what bloody agony! O God, he'd be a mass of dead rotting decay, and she'd still be young and beautiful and alert and desirable, O God, and her life would run on, run on, there'd be all the grief and the sorrowing for her and tears in a cold widowed bed, O God, but the years would run on and she'd still be young and desirable, and somebody else would want her, some youngster, some wangler, and youth and her flesh and life would be clamorous, and her bed would no longer be cold and widowed. O God, God. Something wet ran down his cheek. Not a tear, but the cold clammy sweat from his forehead. God, what agony!

Hanley suddenly sat up. If he was suffering like that, Williams must be suffering, too. Better to get up and pretend to talk than lie and agonise like that. He got out of bed. Williams raised his head:

"What's up. It isn't two, is it?"

The other men looked up, too, showing that neither of them had been asleep. Hanley shivered and rubbed his hands to warm them in the chill dug-out.

"No, only five to twelve. But I couldn't sleep. Hope I don't disturb you. Benson must be relieved in a few minutes," he added inconsequently.

The other three rolled out of bed and stood stretching and rubbing their hands.

"Too cold to sleep in this damned damp place," said one of them.

"What about a drink?"

"If you have it now, you can't have it later on," said Hanley. "Better wait until two."

Williams put on his equipment and helmet and went up to relieve Benson. The others sat on the boxes trying to talk. Benson came down.

"Anything on?" asked Hanley casually.

"Lots of lights, ordinary strafing on their side. A hell of a bombardment from our side."

"Perhaps if they see we've got wind of it, they'll postpone the attack?" suggested the youngest officer.

"Rot," said Benson. "They know jolly well that all this part of the line has been denuded to feed the Fifth Army. They'll attack, all right."

They were silent. Hanley looked at his watch. Five past twelve. How damnably slowly the time went; and yet these were their last minutes on earth. He felt something had to be done.

"Let's have a hand at bridge."

"What, tonight, now?"

"Well, why not? It's no good sitting here grumping like owls, and you don't suggest a prayer meeting, do you?"

The last suggestion was met with oaths of a forcible nature. Hanley cleared the table and threw down the cards.

"Cut for deal."

Just before two, Hanley slipped into his breeches pocket the ten francs he had won, and stood up. He put on trench coat and muffler, tried his broken torch for about the twentieth time, then threw it down disgustedly and fitted on his equipment. The subaltern who was to relieve Williams on trench duty was already dressed and waiting. Hanley put on his hat and turned to the others.

"I'll come round and see you after you've taken up battle positions; but if by any chance I don't see you again – cheerio."

"Cheerio."

They found Williams, his runner, and a sergeant waiting in the trench outside the dug-out entrance.

"Anything doing?"

"Nothing particular. I went on patrol. Their wire's got gaps cut, with knife-rests in the gaps, all the way along."

"Um."

"Lot of signal rockets, too."

"I see. Our artillery seems to have ceased altogether."

"Saving ammunition for the show."

"Be more sensible to strafe now while the Boche is taking up battle positions."

"Oh, well, that's the staff's job, not ours."

Hanley, Williams, the sergeant, two runners, started for the Outpost Line. The trench was drier, the night not so dark, with faint stars mistily gleaming among light clouds. Weather clearing up – just the Boche's luck again. The five men moved along without talking, absorbed partly in a strange anxious preoccupation, partly in keeping upright on the slippery trench. Hanley and Williams, of course, knew the full extent of their danger, had faced the ultimate despair, passed beyond revolt or hope. The sergeant still hoped – that he might be wounded and taken prisoner. The two men only knew they were "in for a show". All were dry-mouthed, a little sickish with apprehension, a little awkward in all their movements; the thought of deserting their posts never even occurred to them.

They passed the three Canadian crosses, distinctly outlined on the quiet sky; then the dragon piece of corrugated iron. At the end of the communication trench they found waiting the men from the four posts, under a sergeant. Hanley spoke in low tones – there might be advance patrols lying just outside their wire.

"All your men present, ser'ant?"

"Yes, sir."

"Right. You know your orders. See that each section joins its own platoon, and then report to your own platoon commander. Don't waste time."

"Very good, sir."

The line of men filed past them in the darkness. For the hundredth time Hanley noticed the curious pathos of fatigue in these silent moving figures – the young bodies somehow tired to age and apathy. When they had gone he took Williams a little aside.

"If I were you, I should see that each of you occupies a separate bay. Get in the first bay yourself, then the runner, then the sergeant. They won't dare try to bolt back past you. Besides – er – there's more chance if you're spread out."

"I was wondering what happens if all three of us are knocked out before the Boche actually gets into the trench, and so no green light is fired?"

"Oh, we must risk that. Besides, there are similar volunteer parties on every company front."

"I see."

"I took a compass bearing from the fire-step outside Company HQ yesterday, so I shan't miss your light. I expect they'll be on us ten minutes later. Perhaps we'll beat off the first two or three attacks."

"Yes. Perhaps."

They were silent. Then Hanley made an effort.

"Well, goodbye, old man. Best of luck."

"Best of luck, goodbye."

They were too shy and English even to shake hands.

It was past three when Hanley and Parker got back to their own line and found the whole company standing to in battle positions. Hanley kept his signallers on the first floor of the big dug-out. He sent off to Battalion Headquarters the code message which meant they were in battle positions and all ready. He took a candle and went down to the lower dug-out, where they had spent so many nights. It looked barer and damper than ever, empty except for the bare sacking beds, the boxes, the table.

Outside in the trench the air was moist and fresh. He took two Very pistols, one loaded with green, one with red, and laid them on either side of him on the parapet. Hanley was at the extreme left of the bay, with two riflemen to his right. Twenty yards to his left was the communication trench leading to the outpost line, now blocked with wire and knife-rests, and guarded by a bombing section.

A signaller came up from the dug-out with a message. Hanley went down and read it by the light of a candle. He noticed the bowed back and absorbed look of a signaller tapping out a message on a Fullerphone. The message he had received simply reiterated the order that their positions were to be held at all costs. Hanley felt angry, screwed up the piece of paper and stuffed it in his pocket. Damn them, how many more times did they think that order had to be given? He returned to the trench, and resumed his watch.

3.50 AM. One battery of German guns languidly firing on back areas – pretence that all was as usual.

3.52 AM. Signal rockets all along the German line. Then silence.

3.55 AM. Two miles to his right a fierce bombardment, stretching over several miles. The battle had begun.

3.57 AM. Two miles to his left another bombardment. The British artillery on their own front opened up a defensive barrage.

4 AM. With a terrific crash, which immediately blotted out the roar of the other bombardments, the German artillery on their own front came into action. Hanley half-recoiled. He had been in several big bombardments, and thought he had experienced the utmost limit of artillery. But this was more tremendous, more hellish, more appalling than anything he had experienced. The trench of the outpost line was one continuous line of red, crashing trench mortars and shells. The communication trench was plastered with five-nines.[1] Shells were falling all along their own line – he heard the sharp cry "Stretcher-bearer" very faintly from somewhere close at hand.

The confusion and horror of a great battle descended on him. The crash of shells, the roar of the guns, the brilliant flashes, the eerie piercing scream of a wounded man, the rattle of the machine-guns, the Lewis guns, the two riflemen beside him madly working the bolts of their rifles and fumbling as with trembling hands they thrust in a fresh clip of cartridges – all somehow perceived, but thrust aside in his intense watch. A green light went up about half a mile to the left, then another a little nearer. Hanley stared more intently in the direction of Williams's post – and found himself saying over and over again without knowing he was saying it: "O God, help him, O God, help him, O God, help him."

Suddenly two green lights appeared, one fired straight up as a signal – probably Williams – the other almost along the ground, as if fired at somebody – probably the runner, wounded or in a panic. Sergeant dead, no doubt – Williams and his

[1] German high-explosive shell fired from a 5.9 artillery piece

runner dead, too, by now. Hanley fired a green light. Two minutes later the British barrage shortened.

Hanley grasped the Very pistol loaded with red. Their turn now.

"Stretcher-bearer, stretcher-bearer!"

Crash! A shell right on their bay.

Hanley staggered and felt a fearful pain in his right knee where a shell splinter had hit him. In the faint light of dawn he saw vaguely that one of the riflemen lay huddled on the fire-step, leaving his rifle still on the parapet; the other man had been blown backwards into the trench, and lay with his feet grimly and ludicrously caught in a torn piece of revetment. His helmet had been knocked from his head.

Faint pops of bombs to his immediate left – they were coming up the communication trench. He peered into the steel-smashed light of dawn, but saw only smoke and the fierce red flash of explosions.

Suddenly, to his left, he saw German helmets coming up the communication trench – they had passed the wire barrier! He looked to his right – a little knot of Germans had got through the wire – a Lewis gun swept them away like flies. He felt the blood running down his leg.

Somebody was standing beside him. A voice, far off, was speaking:

"Bombing attack beaten off, sir."

"Very good, carry on."

"There's only two of us left, sir."

"Carry on."

"Very good, sir."

More Germans on the right; another, longer row coming up the communication trench. Then, suddenly, Germans seemed to spring up in every direction. Hanley fired six shots from his Webley at those in front. He saw others falling hit, or jumping into the trench on either side.

A red light shot up straight in the air. A second later two bombs fell in the bay. A torn, crumpled figure collapsed sideways. The Germans reorganised, while the moppers-up did their job.

# It's Just the Way It Is

# It's Just the Way It Is

**H. E. Bates**

*Second World War*


November rain falls harshly on the clean tarmac, and the wind, turning suddenly, lifts sprays of yellow elm leaves over the black hangars.

The man and the woman, escorted by a sergeant, look very small as they walk by the huge cavernous openings where the bombers are.

The man, who is perhaps fifty and wears a black overcoat and bowler hat, holds an umbrella slantwise over the woman, who is about the same age, but very grey and slow on her feet, so that she is always a pace or two behind the umbrella and must bend her face against the rain.

On the open track beyond the hangars they are caught up by the wind, and are partially blown along, huddled together. Now and then the man looks up at the Stirlings, which protrude over the track, but he looks quickly away again and the woman does not look at all.

"Here we are, sir," the sergeant says at last. The man says "Thank you," but the woman does not speak.

They have come to a long one-storeyed building, painted grey, with "Squadron Headquarters" in white letters on the door. The sergeant opens the door for them and they go in, the man flapping and shaking the umbrella as he. closes it down.

The office of the Wing Commander is at the end of a passage; the sergeant taps on the door, opens it and salutes. As the man and woman follow him, the man first, taking off his hat, the woman hangs a little behind, her face passive.

"Mr and Mrs Shepherd, sir," the sergeant says.

"Oh yes, good afternoon." The sergeant, saluting, closes the door and goes.

"Good afternoon, sir," the man says.

The woman does not speak.

"Won't you please sit down, madam?" the Wing Commander says. "And you too, sir. Please sit down."

He pushes forward two chairs, and slowly the man and the

woman sit down, the man leaning his weight on the umbrella.

The office is small and there are no more chairs. The Wing Commander remains standing, his back resting against a table, beyond which, on the wall, the flight formations are ticketed up.

He is quite young, but his eyes, which are glassy and grey, seem old and focused distantly so that he seems to see far beyond the man and the woman and even far beyond the grey-green Stirlings lined up on the dark tarmac in the rain. He folds his arms across his chest and is glad at last when the man looks up at him and speaks.

"We had your letter, sir. But we felt we should like to come and see you, too."

"I am glad you came."

"I know you are busy, but we felt we must come. We felt you wouldn't mind."

"Not at all. People often come."

"There are just some things we should like to ask you."

"I understand."

The man moves his lips, ready to speak again, but the words do not come. For a moment his lips move like those of someone who stutters, soundlessly, quite helplessly. His hands grip hard on the handle of the umbrella, but still the words do not come and at last it is the Wing Commander who speaks.

"You want to know if everything possible was done to eliminate an accident?"

The man looks surprised that someone should know this, and can only nod his head.

"Everything possible was done."

"Thank you, sir."

"But there are things you can never foresee. The weather forecast may say, for example, no cloud over Germany, for perhaps sixteen hours, but you go over and you find a thick layer of cloud all the way, and you never see your target – and perhaps there is severe icing as you come home."

"Was it like this when——"

"Something like it. You never know. You can't be certain."

Suddenly, before anyone can speak again, the engines of a Stirling close by are revved up to a roar that seems to shake the walls of the room; and the woman looks up, startled, as if terrified that the 'plane will race forward and crash against the windows. The roar of airscrews rises furiously and then falls again, and the sudden rise and fall of sound seems to frighten

21

her into speech.

"Why aren't you certain? Why can't you be certain? He should never have gone out! You must know that! You must know it! You must know that he should never have gone!"

"Please," the man says.

"Day after day you are sending out young boys like this. Young boys who haven't begun to live. Young boys who don't know what life is. Day after day you send them out and they don't come back and you don't care! You don't care!"

She is crying bitterly now and the man puts his arm on her shoulder. She is wearing a fur and he draws it a fraction closer about her neck.

"You don't care, do you! You don't care! It doesn't matter to you. You don't care!"

"Mother," the man says.

Arms folded, the Wing Commander looks at the floor, silently waiting for her to stop. She goes on for a minute or more longer, shouting and crying her words, violent and helpless, until at last she is exhausted and stops. Her fur slips off her shoulder and falls to the ground, and the man picks it up and holds it in his hands, helpless, too.

The Wing Commander walks over to the window and looks out. The airscrews of the Stirling are turning smoothly, shining like steel pin-wheels in the rain, and now, with the woman no longer shouting, the room seems very silent, and finally the Wing Commander walks back across the room and stands in front of the man and woman again.

"You came to ask me something," he says.

"Take no notice, sir. Please. She is upset."

"You want to know what happened? Isn't that it?"

"Yes, sir. It would help us a little, sir."

The Wing Commander says very quietly: "Perhaps I can tell you a little. He was always coming to me and asking to go out on operations. Most of them do that. But he used to come and beg to be allowed to go more than most. So more often than not it was a question of stopping him from going rather than making him go. It was a question of holding him back. You see?"

"Yes, sir."

"And whenever I gave him a trip he was very happy. And the crew were happy. They liked going with him. They liked being together, with him, because they liked him so much and they trusted him. There were seven of them and they were all together."

The woman is listening, slightly lifting her head.

"It isn't easy to tell you what happened on that trip. But we know that conditions got suddenly very bad and that there was bad cloud for a long way. And we know that they had navigational difficulties and that they got a long way off their course.

"Even that might not have mattered, but as they were coming back the outer port engine went. Then the radio transmitter went and the receiver. Everything went wrong. The wireless operator somehow got the transmitter and the receiver going again, but then they ran short of petrol. You see, everything was against him."

"Yes, sir."

"They came back the last hundred miles at about a thousand feet. But they trusted him completely, and he must have known they trusted him. A crew gets like that – flying together gives them this tremendous faith in each other."

"Yes, sir."

"They trusted him to get them home, and he got them home. Everything was against him. He feathered the outer starboard engine and then, in spite of everything, got them down on two engines. It was a very good show. A very wonderful show."

The man is silent, but the woman lifts her head. She looks at the Wing Commander for a moment or two, immobile, very steady, and then says, quite distinctly, "Please tell us the rest."

"There is not much," he says. "It was a very wonderful flight, but they were out of luck. They were up against all the bad luck in the world. When they came to land they couldn't see the flarepath very well, but he got them down. And then, as if they hadn't had enough, they came down slightly off the runway and hit an obstruction. Even then they didn't crash badly. But it must have thrown him and he must have hit his head somewhere with great force, and that was the end."

"Yes, sir. And the others?" the man says.

"They were all right. Even the second pilot. I wish you could have talked to them. It would have helped if you could have talked to them. They know that he brought them home. They know that they owe everything to him."

"Yes, sir."

The Wing Commander does not speak, and the man very

slowly puts the fur over the woman's shoulders. It is like a signal for her to get up, and as she gets to her feet the man stands up too, straightening himself, no longer leaning on the umbrella.

"I haven't been able to tell you much," the Wing Commander says. "It's just the way it is."

"It's everything," the man says.

For a moment the woman still does not speak, but now she stands quite erect. Her eyes are quite clear, and her lips, when she does speak at last, are quite calm and firm.

"I know now that we all owe something to him," she says. "Goodbye."

"Goodbye, madam."

"Goodbye, sir," the man says.

"You are all right for transport?"

"Yes, sir. We have a taxi."

"Good. The sergeant will take you back."

"Goodbye, sir. Thank you."

"Goodbye," the woman says.

"Goodbye."

They go out of the office. The sergeant meets them at the outer door, and the man puts up the umbrella against the rain. They walk away along the wet perimeter, dwarfed once again by the grey-green noses of the Stirlings. They walk steadfastly, almost proudly, and the man holds the umbrella a little higher than before, and the woman, keeping up with him now, lifts her head.

And the Wing Commander, watching them from the window, momentarily holds his face in his hands.

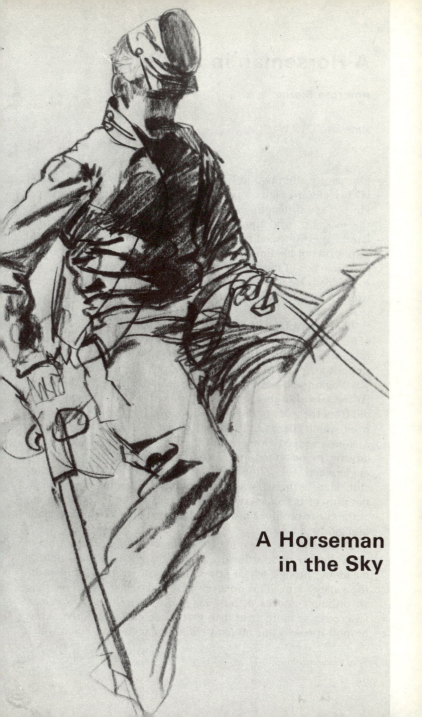

# A Horseman
# in the Sky

# A Horseman in the Sky

**Ambrose Bierce**

*American Civil War*


One sunny afternoon in the autumn of the year 1861, a soldier lay in a clump of laurel by the side of a road in Western Virginia. He lay at full length, upon his stomach, his feet resting upon the toes, his head upon the left forearm. His extended right hand loosely grasped his rifle. But for the somewhat methodical disposition of his limbs and a slight rhythmic movement of the cartridge box at the back of his belt, he might have been thought to be dead. He was asleep at his post of duty. But if detected he would be dead shortly afterward, that being the just and legal penalty of his crime.

The clump of laurel in which the criminal lay was in the angle of a road which, after ascending, southward, a steep acclivity[1] to that point, turned sharply to the west, running along the summit for perhaps one hundred yards. There it turned south-ward again and went zigzagging downward through the forest. At the salient of that second angle was a large flat rock, jutting out from the ridge to the northward, overlooking the deep valley from which the road ascended. The rock capped a high cliff; a stone dropped from its outer edge would have fallen sheer downward one thousand feet to the tops of the pines. The angle where the soldier lay was on another spur of the same cliff. Had he been awake he would have commanded a view, not only of the short arm of the road and the jutting rock but of the entire profile of the cliff below it. It might well have made him giddy to look.

The country was wooded everywhere except at the bottom of the valley to the northward, where there was a small natural meadow, through which flowed a stream scarcely visible from the valley's rim. This open ground looked hardly larger than an ordinary dooryard, but was really several acres in extent. Its green was more vivid than that of the enclosing forest. Away beyond it rose a line of giant cliffs similar to those upon which

---

[1] an ascending slope

we are supposed to stand in our survey of the savage scene, and through which the road had somehow made its climb to the summit. The configuration of the valley, indeed, was such that from our point of observation it seemed entirely shut in, and one could not but have wondered how the road which found a way out of it had found a way into it, and whence came and whither went the waters of the stream that parted the meadow two thousand feet below.

No country is so wild and difficult but men will make it a theatre of war; concealed in the forest at the bottom of that military rat-trap, in which half a hundred men in possession of the exits might have starved an army to submission, lay five regiments of Federal infantry. They had marched all the previous day and night and were resting. At nightfall they would take to the road again, climb to the place where their unfaithful sentinel now slept, and descending the other slope of the ridge, fall upon a camp of the enemy at about midnight. Their hope was to surprise it, for the road led to the rear of it. In case of failure their position would be perilous in the extreme; and fail they surely would should accident or vigilance apprise the enemy of the movement.

The sleeping sentinel in the clump of laurel was a young Virginian named Carter Druse. He was the son of wealthy parents, an only child, and had known such ease and cultivation and high living as wealth and taste were able to command in the mountain country of Western Virginia. His home was but a few miles from where he now lay. One morning he had risen from the breakfast table and said, quietly but gravely: "Father, a Union regiment has arrived at Grafton. I am going to join it."

The father lifted his leonine head, looked at the son a moment in silence, and replied: "Go, Carter, and, whatever may occur, do what you conceive to be your duty. Virginia, to which you are a traitor, must get on without you. Should we both live to the end of the war, we will speak further of the matter. Your mother, as the physician has informed you, is in a most critical condition; at the best she cannot be with us longer than a few weeks, but that time is precious. It would be better not to disturb her."

So Carter Druse, bowing reverently to his father, who returned the salute with a stately courtesy which masked a breaking heart, left the home of his childhood to go soldiering. By conscience

27

and courage, by deeds of devotion and daring, he soon commended himself to his fellows and his officers; and it was to these qualities and to some knowledge of the country that he owed his selection for his present perilous duty at the extreme outpost. Nevertheless, fatigue had been stronger than resolution, and he had fallen asleep. What good or bad angel came in a dream to rouse him from his state of crime who shall say? Without a movement, without a sound, in the profound silence and the languor of the later afternoon, some invisible messenger of fate touched with unsealing finger the eyes of his consciousness – whispered into the ear of his spirit the mysterious awakening word which no human lips have ever spoken, no human memory ever has recalled. He quietly raised his forehead from his arm and looked between the masking stems of the laurels, instinctively closing his right hand about the stock of his rifle.

His first feeling was a keen artistic delight. On a colossal pedestal, the cliff, motionless at the extreme edge of the capping rock and sharply outlined against the sky, was an equestrian statue of impressive dignity. The figure of the man sat the figure of the horse, straight and soldierly, but with the repose of a Grecian god carved in the marble which limits the suggestion of activity. The grey costume harmonised with its aerial background; the metal of accoutrement[1] and caparison[2] was softened and subdued by the shadow; the animal's skin had no points of high light. A carbine, strikingly foreshortened, lay across the pommel of the saddle, kept in place by the right hand grasping it at the "grip"; the left hand, holding the bridle rein, was invisible. In silhouette against the sky, the profile of the horse was cut with the sharpness of a cameo; it looked across the heights of air to the confronting cliffs beyond. The face of the rider, turned slightly to the left, showed only an outline of temple and beard; he was looking downward to the bottom of the valley. Magnified by its lift against the sky and by the soldier's testifying sense of the formidableness of a near enemy, the group appeared of heroic, almost colossal, size.

For an instant Druse had a strange, half-defined feeling that he had slept to the end of the war and was looking upon a noble work of art reared upon that commanding eminence to commemorate the deeds of an heroic past of which he had been an

[1] soldier's outfit, equipment
[2] horse's equipment and trappings

inglorious part. The feeling was dispelled by a slight movement of the group; the horse, without moving its feet, had drawn its body slightly backward from the verge; the man remained immobile as before. Broad awake and keenly alive to the significance of the situation, Druse now brought the butt of his rifle against his cheek by cautiously pushing the barrel forward through the bushes, cocked the piece, and, glancing through the sights, covered a vital spot of the horseman's breast. A touch upon the trigger and all would have been well with Carter Druse. At that instant the horseman turned his head and looked in the direction of his concealed foeman – seemed to look into his very face, into his eyes, into his brave, compassionate heart.

Is it, then, so terrible to kill an enemy in war – an enemy who has surprised a secret vital to the safety of one's self and comrades – an enemy more formidable for his knowledge than all his army for its numbers? Carter Druse grew deathly pale; he shook in every limb, turned faint, and saw the statuesque group before him as black figures, rising, falling, moving unsteadily in arcs of circles in a fiery sky. His hand fell away from his weapon, his head slowly dropped until his face rested on the leaves in which he lay. This courageous gentleman and hardy soldier was near swooning from intensity of emotion.

It was not for long; in another moment his face was raised from earth, his hands resumed their places on the rifle, his forefinger sought the trigger; mind, heart, and eyes were clear, conscience and reason sound. He could not hope to capture that enemy; to alarm him would but send him dashing to his camp with his fatal news. The duty of the soldier was plain: the man must be shot dead from ambush – without warning, without a moment's spiritual preparation, with never so much as an unspoken prayer, he must be sent to his account. But no – there is a hope; he may have discovered nothing – perhaps he is but admiring the sublimity of the landscape. If permitted he may turn and ride carelessly away in the direction whence he came. Surely it will be possible to judge at the instant of his withdrawing whether he knows. It may well be that his fixity of attention – Druse turned his head and looked below, through the deeps of air downward, as from the surface to the bottom of a translucent sea. He saw creeping across the green meadow a sinuous line of figures of men and horses – some foolish commander was permitting the soldiers of his escort to water their beasts in the open, in plain view from a hundred summits!

Druse withdrew his eyes from the valley and fixed them again upon the group of man and horse in the sky, and again it was through the sights of his rifle. But this time his aim was at the horse. In his memory, as if they were a divine mandate, rang the words of his father at their parting: "Whatever may occur, do what you conceive to be your duty." He was calm now. His teeth were firmly but not rigidly closed; his nerves were as tranquil as a sleeping babe's – not a tremor affected any muscle of his body; his breathing, until suspended in the act of taking aim, was regular and slow. Duty had conquered; the spirit had said to the body: "Peace, be still." He fired.

At that moment an officer of the Federal force, who, in a spirit of adventure or in quest of knowledge, had left the hidden *bivouac* in the valley, and, with aimless feet, had made his way to the lower edge of a small open space near the foot of the cliff, was considering what he had to gain by pushing his exploration further. At a distance of a quarter-mile before him, but apparently at a stone's throw, rose from its fringe of pines the gigantic face of rock, towering to so great a height above him that it made him giddy to look up to where its edge cut a sharp, rugged line against the sky. At some distance away to his right it presented a clean, vertical profile against a background of blue sky to a point half of the way down, and of distant hills hardly less blue thence to the tops of the trees at its base. Lifting his eyes to the dizzy altitude of its summit, the officer saw an astonishing sight – a man on horseback riding down into the valley through the air!

Straight upright sat the rider, in military fashion, with a firm seat in the saddle, a strong clutch upon the rein to hold his charger from too impetuous a plunge. From his bare head his long hair streamed upward, waving like a plume. His right hand was concealed in the cloud of the horse's lifted mane. The animal's body was as level as if every hoof stroke encountered the resistant earth. Its motions were those of a wild gallop, but even as the officer looked they ceased, with all the legs thrown sharply forward as in the act of alighting from a leap. But this was a flight!

Filled with amazement and terror by this apparition of a horseman in the sky – half believing himself the chosen scribe of some new Apocalypse,[1] the officer was overcome by the

---

[1] revelation; the revelation of the future to St John the Divine described in the New Testament Book of Revelation

intensity of his emotions; his legs failed him and he fell. Almost at the same instant he heard a crashing sound in the trees – a sound that died without an echo, and all was still.

The officer rose to his feet, trembling. The familiar sensation of an abraded shin recalled his dazed faculties. Pulling himself together, he ran rapidly obliquely away from the cliff to a point a half-mile from its foot; thereabout he expected to find his man; and thereabout he naturally failed. In the fleeting instant of his vision his imagination had been so wrought upon by the apparent grace and ease and intention of the marvellous performance that it did not occur to him that the line of march of aerial cavalry is directed downward, and that he could find the objects of his search at the very foot of the cliff. A half hour later he returned to camp.

This officer was a wise man; he knew better than to tell an incredible truth. He said nothing of what he had seen. But when the commander asked him if in his scout he had learned anything of advantage to the expedition, he answered:

"Yes, sir; there is no road leading down into this valley from the southward."

The commander, knowing better, smiled.

After firing his shot Private Carter Druse reloaded his rifle and resumed his watch. Ten minutes had hardly passed when a Federal sergeant crept cautiously to him on hands and knees. Druse neither turned his head nor looked at him, but lay without motion or sign of recognition.

"Did you fire?" the sergeant whispered.

"Yes."

"At what?"

"A horse. It was standing on yonder rock – pretty far out. You see it is no longer there. It went over the cliff."

The man's face was white but he showed no other sign of emotion. Having answered, he turned away his face and said no more. The sergeant did not understand.

"See here, Druse," he said, after a moment's silence, "it's no use making a mystery. I order you to report. Was there anybody on the horse?"

"Yes."

"Who?"

"My father."

The sergeant rose to his feet and walked away "Good God!" he said.

# The Drummer Boy of Shiloh

# The Drummer Boy of Shiloh

**Ray Bradbury**

*American Civil War*

In the April night, more than once, blossoms fell from the orchard trees and lighted with rustling taps on the drumhead. At midnight a peach stone left miraculously on a branch through winter, flicked by a bird, fell swift and unseen; it struck once, like panic, and jerked the boy upright. In silence he listened to his own heart ruffle away, away – at last gone from his eyes and back in his chest again.

After that he turned the drum on its side, where its great lunar face peered at him whenever he opened his eyes.

His face, alert or at rest, was solemn. It was a solemn time and a solemn night for a boy just turned fourteen in the peach orchard near Owl Creek not far from the church at Shiloh.

" ... thirty-one ... thirty-two ... thirty-three." Unable to see, he stopped counting.

Beyond the thirty-three familiar shadows forty thousand men, exhausted by nervous expectation and unable to sleep for romantic dreams of battles yet unfought, lay crazily askew in their uniforms. A mile farther on, another army was strewn helter-skelter, turning slowly, basting themselves with the thought of what they would do when the time came – a leap, a yell, a blind plunge their strategy, raw youth their protection and benediction.

Now and again the boy heard a vast wind come up that gently stirred the air. But he knew what it was – the army here, the army there, whispering to itself in the dark. Some men talking to others, others murmuring to themselves, and all so quiet it was like a natural element arisen from South or North with the motion of the earth toward dawn.

What the men whispered the boy could only guess and he guessed that it was "Me, I'm the one, I'm the one of all the rest who won't die. I'll live through it. I'll go home. The band will play. And I'll be there to hear it."

*Yes,* thought the boy, *that's all very well for them, they can give as good as they get.*

34

For with the careless bones of the young men, harvested by night and bundled around campfires, were the similarly strewn steel bones of their rifles with bayonets fixed like eternal lightning lost in the orchard grass.

*Me,* thought the boy, *I got only a drum, two sticks to beat it and no shield.*

There wasn't a man-boy on this ground tonight who did not have a shield he cast, riveted or carved himself on his way to his first attack, compounded of remote but none the less firm and fiery family devotion, flag-blown patriotism and cocksure immortality strengthened by the touchstone of very real gunpowder, ramrod, Minie ball[1] and flint. But without these last, the boy felt his family move yet farther off in the dark, as if one of those great prairie-burning trains had chanted them away, never to return – leaving him with this drum which was worse than a toy in the game to be played tomorrow or someday much too soon.

The boy turned on his side. A moth brushed his face, but it was peach blossom. A peach blossom flicked him, but it was a moth. Nothing stayed put. Nothing had a name. Nothing was as it once was.

If he stayed very still, when the dawn came up and the soldiers put on their bravery with their caps, perhaps they might go away, the war with them, and not notice him lying small here, no more than a toy himself.

"Well, by thunder now," said a voice. The boy shut his eyes to hide inside himself, but it was too late. Someone, walking by in the night, stood over him. "Well," said the voice quietly, "here's a soldier crying *before* the fight. Good. Get it over. Won't be time once it all starts."

And the voice was about to move on when the boy, startled, touched the drum at his elbow. The man, above, hearing this stopped. The boy could feel his eyes, sense him slowly bending near. A hand must have come down out of the night, for there was a little *rat-tat* as the fingernails brushed and the man's breath fanned the boy's face.

"Why, it's the drummer boy, isn't it?"

The boy nodded, not knowing if his nod was seen.

"Sir, is that you?" he said.

"I assume it is." The man's knees cracked as he bent still

---

[1] an elongated bullet which expanded when fired

closer. He smelled as all fathers should smell, of salt-sweat, tobacco, horse and boot leather, and the earth he walked upon. He had many eyes. No, not eyes, brass buttons that watched the boy.

He could only be, and was, the general. "What's your name, boy?" he asked.

"Joby, sir" whispered the boy, starting to sit up.

"All right, Joby, don't stir." A hand pressed his chest gently, and the boy relaxed. "How long you been with us, Joby?"

"Three weeks, sir."

"Run off from home or join legitimate, boy?"

Silence.

"Damn-fool question," said the general. "Do you shave yet, boy? Even more of a fool. There's your cheek, fell right off the tree overhead. And the others here, not much older. Raw, raw, damn raw, the lot of you. You ready for tomorrow or the next day, Joby?"

"I think so, sir."

"You want to cry some more, go on ahead. I did the same last night."

"You sir?"

"God's truth. Thinking of everything ahead. Both sides figuring the other side will just give up, and soon, and the war done in weeks and us all home. Well, that's not how it's going to be. And maybe that's why I cried."

"Yes, sir," said Joby.

The general must have taken out a cigar now, for the dark was suddenly filled with the Indian smell of tobacco unlighted yet, but chewed as the man thought what next to say.

"It's going to be a crazy time," said the general. "Counting both sides, there's a hundred thousand men – give or take a few thousand – out there tonight, not one as can spit a sparrow off a tree, or knows a horse clod from a Minie ball. Stand up, bare the breast, ask to be a target, thank them and sit down, that's us, that's them. We should turn tail and train four months, they should do the same. But here we are, taken with Spring fever and thinking it blood lust, taking our sulphur with cannons instead of with molasses, as it should be – going to be a hero, going to live forever. And I can see all them over there nodding agreement, save the other way around. It's wrong. boy. It's wrong as a head put on hindside front and a man marching backward through life. Sometime this week more innocents will get shot out of pure Cherokee enthusiasm than ever got shot before. Owl Creek was full of boys splashing around in the noonday sun just a few hours ago. I fear it will be full of boys again, just floating, at sundown tomorrow, not caring where the current takes them."

The general stopped and made a little pile of winter leaves and twigs in the dark as if he might at any moment strike fire to them to see his way through the coming days when the sun might not show its face because of what was happening here and just beyond.

The boy watched the hand stirring the leaves and opened his lips to say something, but did not say it. The general heard the boy's breath and spoke himself.

"Why am I telling you this? That's what you wanted to ask, eh? Well, when you got a bunch of wild horses on a loose rein somewhere, somehow you got to bring order, rein them in. These lads, fresh out of the milkshed, don't know what I know; and I can't tell them – men actually die in war. So each is his own army. I got to make one army of them. And for that, boy, I need you."

"Me!" the boy's lips barely twitched.

"You, boy," said the general quietly. "You are the heart of the army. Think about that. You are the heart of the army. Listen to me, now."

And lying there, Joby listened. And the general spoke. If he, Joby, beat slow tomorrow, the heart would beat slow in the men. They would lag by the wayside. They would drowse in the fields on their muskets. They would sleep forever after that – in those same fields, their hearts slowed by a drummer boy and stopped by enemy lead.

But if he beat a sure, steady, ever faster rhythm, then, then, their knees would come up in a long line down over that hill, one knee after the other, like a wave on the ocean shore. Had he seen the ocean ever? Seen the waves rolling in like a well-ordered cavalry charge to the sand? Well, that was it. That's what he wanted, that's what was needed. Joby was his right hand and his left. He gave the orders, but Joby set the pace.

So bring the right knee up and the right foot out and the left knee up and the left foot out, one following the other in good time, in brisk time. Move the blood up the body and make the head proud and the spine stiff and the jaw resolute. Focus the eye and set the teeth, flare the nostrils and tighten the hands,

37

put steel armour all over the men, for blood moving fast in them does indeed make men feel as if they'd put on steel. He must keep at it, at it! Long and steady, steady and long! Then, even though shot or torn, those wounds got in hot blood – in blood he'd helped stir – would feel less pain. If their blood was cold, it would be more than slaughter, it would be murderous nightmare and pain best not told and no one to guess.

The general spoke and stopped, letting his breath slack off. Then, after a moment, he said, "So there you are, that's it. Will you do that, boy? Do you know now you're general of the army when the general's left behind?"

The boy nodded mutely.

"You'll run them through for me then, boy?"

"Yes, sir!"

"Good. And, God willing, many nights from tonight, many years from now, when you're as old or far much older than me, when they ask you what you did in this awful time, you will tell them – one part humble and one part proud – I was the drummer boy at the battle of Owl Creek or the Tennessee River, or maybe they'll just name it after the church there. I was the drummer boy at Shiloh. Good grief, that has a beat and sound to it fitting for Mr Longfellow. 'I was the drummer boy at Shiloh.' Who will ever hear those words and not know you, boy, or what you. thought this night, or what you'll think to-morrow or the next day when we must get up on our legs and move."

The general stood up. "Well, then. God bless you, boy. Good night."

"Good night, sir." And tobacco, brass, boot polish, salt-sweat and leather, the man moved away through the grass.

Joby lay for a moment staring, but unable to see where the man had gone. He swallowed. He wiped his eyes. He cleared his throat. He settled himself. Then, at last, very slowly and firmly he turned the drum so it faced up toward the sky.

He lay next to it, his arm around it, feeling the tremor, the touch, the muted thunder as all the rest of the April night in the year 1862, near the Tennessee River, not far from the Owl Creek, very close to the church named Shiloh, the peach blossoms fell on the drum.

# Looking for Annie

# Looking for Annie

**Charles Causley**

*Second World War*

During the first four years I was in the navy, I was easily the worst sailor in the fleet. As soon as I got in, I discovered that I was one of those people who suffered from sea-sickness. I often used to wonder why I had joined the navy at all.

Being a Cornishman, of course, may have had something to do with it. I suppose I thought at the time that all Cornishmen "belonged", as we say, to go to sea. That is, if they didn't join the then Duke of Cornwall's Light Infantry. But my father had been in the trenches in France in the First World War, and from what I'd heard about it, I didn't fancy the army. Another thing: when I was about eight I went to stay with my Auntie Elsie for a summer holiday, and she lived near an army barracks. I can still hear the non-commissioned officers bawling at the recruits on that dusty parade-ground. Not for me, I thought.

The sailors I'd seen ashore in Cornwall, and on the streets of Plymouth, on the other hand, were a different matter. They all seemed to my childlike vision to be strong, smart, handsome, healthy, merry. I thought that if ever I put on that magic uniform, my dough-like complexion, thin arms and legs, spectacles, and general incapacity for games and doing anything remotely practical would all fade away and that I should somehow become as they were.

Further, such was my general state of arrested development and full-flowering ignorance, when the war finally did come in my nineteenth year, I thought that if I opted for the navy I should be based in Devonport and that I would be able to get home to Cornwall at weekends. As it turned out, I spent only ten days in what to me was the hell's kitchen of the barracks in six years, and those were ten days too many. Another thing: the one element I failed to take account of when I joined the navy was the sea. But once I was in, it was too late to bother about reasons. Early in 1940 I was drafted to HMS *Sunburst*.

The ship was stationed about as far from Cornwall as it

could possibly be while still in the British Isles. I can see myself now being welcomed by the coxswain, a huge puffy man with warts and a thin spiky beard sticking out like the rays of the sun all round his face as I stood anxiously with my kit-bag and hammock on the heaving slippery narrow steel deck of the destroyer in the green sea of Scapa.

"Name?" growled the coxswain. My arrival had interrupted his tea.

"Trethewey," I squeaked. "D/JX 197950. Ordinary Coder."

The coxswain looked at me like a scientist across whose microscope some fabled insect has suddenly crawled.

"Ordinary *what*?" he said.

"Coder, sir," I said. "Decoding and deciphering signals. It's a new branch."

"Never 'eard of it," said the coxswain. "You're in Number Two Mess. That's the watch-keepers' mess, down forrard. You'll find it. Abandon ship station: Carley Float Number Four, port-side. And remind the Leadin' 'and o' the mess we're sailin' in 'alf an hour. Seventeen-thirty. All right?"

Dismally I gathered up my kit-bag and hammock and trudged forrard.

"Oh, an' – what's s-yer-name!" the coxswain called after me.

"Sir?" I said.

"You want a shave."

I did, too. I hadn't had a proper wash for three days, and it felt like three years. I was so miserable it's a wonder I didn't take a jump over the side. But I'm glad I didn't, because if I had I should never have met Annie.

There he was: down in the mess, sitting on the end of a form under the radio speaker, drinking grey tea made with thick, condensed milk and reading the births and deaths column in an old copy of the *North Cornwall Echo*.

Naturally, Annie wasn't his real name. Annie was called Mark Annear, and he came from the fishing village of Port Treloar on the long, sandy estuary of the River Polwenner that runs off Bodmin Moor into the sea on the north coast of Cornwall. "Annie", of course, came from his surname: Annear. Nobody in Cornwall, or anywhere else in the West Country for that matter, would have dared to call him this. It would have outraged politeness, propriety. In the navy, though, with its passion for nicknames, it was inevitable, but had nothing whatever to do with personal characteristics. "Hookey" Walker,

"Dolly" Grey, "Bungy" Williams, "Clara" Bow, "Brigham" Young, were all attached as automatically as official numbers. "Annie" Annear was a name I heard nowhere else but in *Sunburst*. Most important, he didn't appear to mind the nickname. Anyhow, I remember thinking, when I first heard it, that it was wildly inappropriate.

He was, in those days, a man of about twenty-six: tall, hefty, very big-boned. His wrists and fingers seemed to me to be constructed on an entirely larger, looser principle from my own. To look at, Annie was by no means what many people take to be a typical Cornishman. He wasn't short, thick-set, dark-haired, Celtic-eyed. Yet his Cornish surname – Annear – should have given me a clue: it comes from *an hir*, the tall or the long. His height, his large, open, freckled face and sandy thatch of hair was something you would expect to find on the prairies of Canada or on the sheep-farms of Australia, not in his father's boat-building yard at Port Treloar.

As I scrambled down the metal ladder the rest of the members of the mess – arguing, scuffling, singing, writing, playing uckers (ludo), even somebody shaving – ignored me. But Annie picked up my kit-bag. "Hello," he said in a slow, easy West Country voice. "My name's Mark Annear. Supply Assistant. I'm in the stores. Everybody calls me Annie. Have some tea. Shockin' stuff, but there's nothing else."

After the unexpected greeting in familiar Cornish tones, I began to feel that life in the *Sunburst* mightn't be so bad after all. It was, of course. I might have known what to expect from the boat journey between the mainland at Thurso and Lyness. I seemed to be the only person on board being ill. It was quite a fine day in early summer, and, to make things worse, I was the only passenger in naval uniform. A priest and a couple of young children paused in a ball game and gazed at me with some concern: not so much, I imagine, for me as for the future of the country.

If the passenger-boat was bad, the *Sunburst* was worse. Apart from rolling, she used to leap forward like an electric hare, and – shut as we were inside – we would seem for a short while to be in some kind of spaceship on our way to the moon. Then she would suddenly change her role. Like a miners' cage, she would drop flat on the sea with a dreadful metallic bang that seemed to rattle every separate screw and nut and bolt in the ship. It was terrifying; something out of a flooding Inferno.

And, naturally, my sea-sickness didn't get any better.

Everybody, especially the new hands who knew nothing about it, was full of advice. Lie down, close your eyes, drink cold water, they said. It's a sort of spirit-level in your ears: keep them steady. Stand up. Sit amidships with your back to something warm. Keep your eyes open. Don't look at the sea. Keep working, and (this was a favourite one) it's your imagination. I resorted to rum, pills, fasting, injections, prayer. All no good. I just went on being ill. The only person who didn't give me the benefit of his opinion was Annie. In fact, he never mentioned sea-sickness.

Annie had almost only one topic of conversation: the fishing village of Port Treloar where he lived. Up to the outbreak of war, he had spent all his life around the bay and the estuary there, working for his father, and sailing. One day he produced a faded photograph of himself. The resemblance wasn't a good one, and it was badly out of focus: Annie, grasping a tiller with giant paws and gazing sternly but dimly from the cardboard. Nevertheless, that photograph – obviously – was a talisman; a reminder of another reality. "You must come and see me," he said. "And my wife. You can get a train from Dunborough. Change at Port Isaac. When you get to Port Treloar, come across on the ferry. It's a motor-boat; Tom Hocken runs it. At least, he did when I was home last: that's eight months ago. When you get to the other side of the river, our boat-building yard's facing you. 'Denzil Annear and Son' – that's me – 'Boat Builders, Port Treloar'. Blue letters on a white ground; you can see it for half a mile. There's a steep hill, and about a hundred yards up on the left is our house. It's whitewashed. You can't miss it; it's the only one on that side. Come any time."

"I will, Annie," I said. "It sounds all right."

"It *is* all right," he said. "Of course, I don't use the ferry. I row over in my own boat. Got a little boat-house almost underneath the landing-stage. I keep my things there. Funny, my boat's tied up on the other side of the river waiting for me now. And I'm here. In Freetown. Don't know how long she'll have to wait."

I laughed; but Annie looked serious. "And don't wait till the end of the war," he went on. "Anyhow, it looks like going on for ever."

"Supposing you're not at home?" I said.

"Doesn't matter," said Annie. "I've written home about you.

By the way, my wife's expecting. Perhaps you'll see the baby before I do. You never know."

I never forgot that conversation with Annie. We were sitting outside the canteen by the King Tom Jetty at Freetown. Just then the liberty-boat came in, and by the time we returned to the ship it was quite dark. The coxswain was waiting for me on the gangway.

"Trethewey, Ordinary Coder?" he said, giving me that old scientific look.

"Sir?" I said.

"You're going on draft. Tonight," he said.

"Ashore, Cox?" I said hopefully: white man's grave or no white man's grave.

"The *Lifton*. Cruiser. Shake yer up," he said encouragingly. "Boat'll be 'ere for yer in twenty minutes. Git flyin'." And he vanished back into his office like a wicked fairy.

Annie helped me pack my kit-bag and lash my spare books in my hammock. In an hour, I had left the *Sunburst* for ever and was in the *Lifton*, making for Simonstown, Fremantle, Sydney, the Pacific. Years later, I heard that the *Sunburst* had stayed in Freetown three weeks, then returned to Londonderry.

Annie and I wrote a letter or two. But he wasn't what might be called a writing man. And I was often too ill, too far away, to bother. Anything might have happened to him. It was a long war for those who had been at sea since 1939. One Christmas – it must have been in Brisbane, we were there four days in 1943 – I nearly sent him a cable. But it seemed, at the last minute, absurd. He might have been dead. I had heard that the *Sunburst* had been at Crete. So I didn't really think much more about Annie until nearly a year later.

I was home in Cornwall, at Dunborough, on forty-eight days leave. I was tired of people asking me when I was going back, and telling me how thin I was. Secretly, I was worried about my next draft. I'd left the *Lifton* and was wondering how long my inside would last if I went back to destroyers. So, to take my mind off it, I decided to go down to Port Treloar and find Annie.

Once I got started, I couldn't help wondering why I hadn't gone before. The feeling of excitement, of expectancy, soon wore off, though. I began to wish I'd stayed at home. The train rattled along the tiny branch line past scruffy little fields, mud, bare trees. It was beastly cold November weather, and I felt it pretty badly after three years in the Pacific. The railway line hugged the coast, and now and then, through the mist, you could catch a sight of the grey, cold heaving line of the north Cornish sea. Dreadful. There was practically nobody else on the train. Increasingly, I wished I hadn't come, and began to wonder how I was going to get back to Dunborough that night. Looking for Annie! Annie was probably dead; comfortable at the bottom of some ocean. And what should I say to his wife?

The train stopped violently, as though we had hit something. The wind from the sea came sawing up the platform like a blade of ragged ice. I pulled my coat about me and wished for the fiftieth time I'd worn my uniform. So this was Port Treloar.

It was just as Annie had described it. Climbing into the motor-boat to cross the river, five minutes later, I felt I had known Tom Hocken for years. "Mr Hocken?" I said. Like many Cornish people dealing with a supposed foreigner, he professed to show no surprise. "Everybody d'knaw me," he said, and we shot in a thick spray of muddy water across the estuary. I spent the journey mopping my face and my thin coat. I was the only passenger. As I got out of the boat on the other side, I thought I would try again. "A friend," I said, "told me about you. In Africa, Mr Hocken."

"That'll be sixpence," he said. "Look slippy out o' the boat now, my sonny. I got to be on t'other side in a few minutes."

I gave up, gave him the money, stepped on the wooden jetty. I was absolutely alone. The mist and the rain were still blowing in from the sea; and the sea itself was now invisible. I could hardly see the houses on the other side of the river. I might have been a traveller on the landscape of an unknown planet. Then I noticed the signboard.

There it was: painted in blue and white. "Denzil Annear and Son. Boat Builders. Port Treloar." Just as Annie had said. My throat seemed to close up. I felt, surprisingly, that I might easily burst into tears. But a voice startled me from my line of thought.

"You came, then," it said: and laughed. There was no mistaking that easy, West Country voice. I looked down from the jetty to the edge of the river beneath me. There, standing in a rowing-boat and tying her up, was Annie. He wore his naval uniform, a thick scarf, gloves, and – I remember thinking this rather odd – a balaclava helmet. At the bottom of the boat was a black, wooden box with his name and number painted on it in white. He must have crossed the river behind us.

"Annie!" I shouted. He laughed again and looked up at me, the mist swirling round his legs.

"Just like you to choose today," he said. "Go on up to the house and break the news I'm coming, will you? I've got to unlock the boat-house and get this box up the ladder."

"Can I help you?" I said.

"You'll break your neck, boy," he grinned. "I remember the day you joined the mess in *Sunburst*. The house is a hundred yards up the hill, on the left. Remember? And how's your stomach? I'll see you in ten minutes. Oh, and welcome to Port Treloar!"

He hopped out of the boat, balanced on some narrow stone steps, put his hand through an aperture in the top of the door, and drew out a large, flat key. I set off up the hill.

Almost as soon as I'd lifted the iron knocker, the door opened. It was Annie's wife all right. I recognized her at once from the photographs I'd seen. She was a tall girl, with a pale, milk-white face, and red hair. And she showed no surprise at seeing me. Her face didn't move at all, either with pleasure or sorrow. She looked like someone still recovering, slowly, from some long illness. "You're a friend of Mark's," she said. "Come in."

She led the way into a tiny kitchen. There was a fire burning and a kettle boiling. "Have a cup of tea," she said. "It's a long journey. You're Richard Trethewey, aren't you? Mark used to write about you in his letters from the *Sunburst*. Mark made a lot of friends."

"Did Annie . . . that is, Mark . . . tell you that he almost saved my life?" I said. She laughed, and her face lit up wonderfully. "That's right," she said. "That's what they used to call him in the navy. Annie. Annie Annear. I've had a lot of visitors since . . . since . . . ."

An awful premonition came over me. I suddenly felt as though I might, quite quickly, become desperately ill: even die. I put down my cup of tea and stood up.

"You've had a lot of visitors since what?" I said. There was a little scuffle at the door. She went to it, opened it; brought in a small boy of about four, the image of Annie, and holding an eyeless teddy-bear. The child gazed at me solemnly, smiled faintly, clutched his mother's hand, leaned against her. "Don't you know?" she said. There was a pause. "Mark . . . Annie, as you call him . . . was lost at sea two years ago. He was in the

*Sunburst.* They were in an anti-submarine patrol covering a convoy in the Barents Sea, somewhere off the North Cape. The ship simply sailed off into the blue and disappeared. No signal. Nothing. I had a letter from the Admiralty, but it didn't tell me much. I thought you knew. Annie's dead."

My hands began to shake so much that I put them in my pockets. I sat down. My stomach seemed to turn to lead, to roll completely over like a ship in a heavy sea. For a few seconds, I could hardly breathe. I felt as though, for a terrifying moment, I'd been provided with a new inside. Then I said, "Are you prepared for a shock?"

She looked at me with complete calm. "Nothing can shock me now," she said, and adjusted one of the little boy's socks. "Listen," I said. "When I came up from the ferry just now, Mark – your husband – Annie – was tying up his boat down there. He'll be here in a minute. It was misty; raining. I spoke to him."

I must say that Annie's wife was an amazing girl. She simply looked at me like a mother who has to comfort a feverish child. "Have another cup of tea," she said. "It's the shock. You were very fond of Mark, weren't you? Do you know, for nearly a year, when I was here with the baby, I fancied I could hear him coming up from the river."

"Are you telling me," I said, "that I've seen a ghost?"

"Cornwall's a funny old place," she said. "I shouldn't think about what you've seen."

I stood up and began to shout. "But I saw him standing up in his boat by the jetty! He had a black box with his name painted on it. He was in uniform and – yes! – a balaclava! *I tell you I saw him!*" And all the time that girl just looked at me and smiled, cool as you like, as if to say: you'll get over it in a moment.

And so I did. And so did she. For the next second, the door opened and in walked Annie, carrying the box. Of the three of us, including the little boy, I don't know who was the most astonished.

You see, I hadn't seen a ghost down at the ferry. It really was Annie. And he really had been posted as missing for two years. The *Sunburst* had been torpedoed off the North Cape, and the German submarine had picked up three survivors: among them, Annie. They had given them a little food and brandy and set them adrift again in one of the leaking ship's boats. Late the following night they had been picked up by some Lapp fishermen and landed on a tiny island north-west of Point Kenahay. Annie's two companions had died, and for over a year he had been unable to speak, from the shock and the cold, and had been nursed by the Lapps. Then they took him by sledge to a Russian hospital on the Kola Peninsula. When he had recovered, and could walk and speak again, he waited for a convoy. In six months, he was back in Belfast. They had flown him to Devonport; then to the nearby Royal Naval Air Station at St Petherwin. Annie had come the last three miles from the air station in a furniture van. "Look at me!" he cried, embracing us all. "I'm a blooming Eskimo!"

And that's almost all there is to it. Annie survived the war all right, and is still building boats down at Port Treloar. As for myself, I was completely changed after that jolt to my stomach when I thought I'd seen Annie's ghost. That was in 1944. I spent the last year of the war bouncing about in a cor-vette: the *Thistle*. And, do you know, I was never sea-sick once. So if you want a really reliable cure for sea-sickness, I suggest that you come down to Cornwall and start looking for Annie.

# A Mystery of Heroism

# A Mystery of Heroism

**Stephen Crane**

*American Civil War*

The dark uniforms of the infantry soldiers were so coated with dust that they seemed almost a part of the clay bank which protected them from the enemy shells. On top of the bank a gun battery was arguing in great roars with enemy guns. When a gun was fired, a red streak as round as a log flashed low in the sky, like a huge bolt of lightning.

One of the infantrymen, Fred Collins, of A Company, was saying, "Thunder! I wish I had a drink. Ain't there any water around here?" Then somebody yelled, "There goes the bugler!"

The eyes of the regiment turned and saw in an instant a picture of a leaping horse and a rider leaning back with a crooked arm and spread fingers before his face. An enemy shell exploded on the ground, with flames shooting out in straight lines. A glittering bugle swung clear as the horse and rider fell. A burning smell filled the air.

Sometimes the soldiers looked down on a little field below them. Its long green grass was rippling gently in a breeze. Beyond it was a gray house half torn to pieces by shells. The line of an old fence was now dimly marked by long weeds and a post here and there. Little ribbons of grey smoke showed where a barn had been.

From beyond a curtain of green woods there came the sound of scuffling, as though two huge animals were fighting. Now and then there could be seen swift-moving men, horses, batteries, and flags. There were rifle shots out there and sometimes wild cheers.

In the middle of all the noise, Smith and Ferguson, two privates of A Company, were arguing.

One of the soldiers in the gun battery on the hill was suddenly smashed down by an enemy shell. His fellow soldiers, trying to get out of the way of danger, tramped over his lifeless body.

A lieutenant of the battery passed the infantrymen. He held his right arm carefully in his left hand. His horse went by them slowly. The officer's face was dirty and sweaty. He smiled grimly when the men stared at him.

Collins of Company A said, "I wish I had a drink. I bet there's water in that old well yonder."

"Yes, but how you going to get it?"

The little field between them and the well was being blasted with enemy shells. Its green and beautiful calm had disappeared. Brown earth was being flung up in large chunks by the shells. The tiny blades of grass were being torn and burned.

The wounded officer, who was now riding over this field, said to himself, "Why, they couldn't shoot any harder if the whole army was here."

A shell struck the ruined house. The last wall fell.

The shells were bursting around the battery on the hill. Fewer men were up there. The horses that pulled the big guns had to stand there. Many had been hit. The men of the infantry could see one animal raising its wounded body with its front legs, and turning its nose to the sky.

Some fellow soldiers were teasing Collins about his thirst. "Well, if you want a drink so bad, why don't you go get it?"

"Well, I will in a minute, if you don't shut up!"

A lieutenant of artillery came down the hill. He passed the colonel of the infantry and threw a fast salute. "We've got to get out of that," he roared angrily. He was a black-bearded man, and his eyes sparkled like those of an insane man. His horse sped by.

A fat infantry major looked after him and laughed. "He's going back to get new orders. If he don't get back with them pretty soon, there will be no battery left."

One of the officers told the colonel that the enemy's infantry would probably attack soon. The colonel paid no attention.

A private looked out over the field and said, "Look there!" The men saw the wounded officer from the battery who had started over the field a short time before. A shell had exploded near him. He lay face down over the body of his dead horse. Shells still crashed around him.

There was an argument in A Company. Collins was shaking his fist at the others. "I ain't afraid to go. If you keep talking, I will go!"

"Of course, you will! You'll run through that field, won't you?"

Collins said in a terrible voice, "You see now!"

The others laughed.

Collins gave them a scowl and went to his captain. The captain was talking to the colonel.

"Captain," said Collins, saluting. "Captain, I ask permission to go get some water from that well over yonder."

The colonel and the captain stared across the field to the well. The captain laughed. "You must be pretty thirsty, Collins."

"Yes, sir, I am."

"Well – ah," said the captain. After a moment, he asked, "Can't you wait?"

"No, sir."

"Look here, my lad," said the colonel (Collins was not a lad), "don't you think that's taking pretty big risks for a little drink of water?"

"I don't know," said Collins uncomfortably. His anger towards his buddies was beginning to fade. "I don't know whether it is."

The colonel and the captain looked at him for a while.

"Well," said the captain finally.

"Well," said the colonel, "if you want to go, why, go."

Collins said, "Much obliged."

As he moved away, the colonel called after him, "Take some of the other men's canteens, and hurry back, now."

"Yes, sir, I will."

The colonel and the captain looked at each other. It suddenly came to them that they could not tell whether Collins wanted to go or not.

Then they turned to watch Collins as he returned to his friends. They pounded Collins's back. The colonel said, "Well, by thunder! I guess he's going."

Collins looked like a man dreaming. He was silent as his friends talked excitedly.

Suddenly he strode away from them. He was swinging five or six canteens by their cords. It seemed as if his cap wouldn't remain firmly on his head. Often he had to reach up and pull it down over his brow.

Four hundred eyes were on him.

"Well, if that ain't the darndest thing! I never thought Fred Collins had the blood in him for that kind of business."

"What's he going to do, anyhow?"

"He's going to that well there after water."

"We ain't dying of thirst, are we? That's foolishness."

"Well, somebody put him up to it, and he's doing it."

When Collins faced the field he had to cross, he became aware of what he had done. He had been led by strange emotions. Now he was under an obligation to walk squarely up to the face of death.

But he wasn't sure he wished to back out, even if he could do so without shame. As a matter of fact, he was sure of very little. He was mainly surprised.

He wondered why he did not feel fear cutting him like a knife. He had been taught that men should feel afraid of certain things, and that men who did not feel this fear were . . . heroes.

He was, then, a hero. On realising it, he felt disappointment. Him, a hero? Then heroes weren't so much.

No, it could not be true. He was not a hero. Heroes had no shames in their lives. As for him, he remembered borrowing fifteen dollars from a friend; he had promised to pay it back the next day, but avoided his friend for ten months. When, back on the farm, his mother had woken him early, he often was angry and childish. His mother had died since he had come to the war.

He now had walked about thirty steps into the field. The regiment was watching him.

From the forest on the other side of the field appeared a small group of men. They fired fiercely at the distant bushes. A sergeant fell flat as if he had slipped on ice.

Collins could see nothing but the red arrows of the shells exploding around him. He made a mad rush for the well.

Rifle bullets now were mixed in with the shells. The air was torn in all directions by hootings, yells, howls.

When he reached the well, he flung himself down and stared into the darkness. He grabbed a canteen, and, unfastening its cap, swung it down by the cord. It hit water and sank. He heard the water flowing into the canteen with a gurgle.

Now he was suddenly struck with the terror of it all. All the power faded from his muscles. He felt like a dead man.

The canteen filled slowly. In a few minutes, he had gotten back his strength and he cursed at it. As he leaned over to yell at the canteen, he saw his eyes reflected like two pieces of metal.

Shells exploded in the distance. Red light shone through the boiling smoke. Collins jerked up the canteen as if his arm had been in a fire.

He jumped up and glared around. On the ground near him lay the old well bucket, with a length of rusty chain. He lowered it into the well. The bucket sank. His hands trembling, he hauled it out. Then he started back to his friends.

His face was white with fear as he ran. He expected a shell to smash him to pieces. He saw the regiment looking at him so far away.

The artillery officer who had fallen in the field minutes before made groans. These small cries, wrenched from him by pain, were heard only by shells and bullets. When wild-eyed Collins came running, this officer raised himself. He was going to give some long, loud cry to ease his torture. But he controlled his face and called, "Say, young man, give me a drink of water, will you?"

"I can't!" Collins screamed in his fear. He ran on, his cap off and his hair flying.

The officer's head sank down and one elbow crooked. One leg was pinned under his dead horse.

But Collins turned. He came dashing back. His face had now turned grey, and in his eyes was all terror. "Here it is! Here it is!"

The officer lay like a drunk. His arm bent like a twig. He was sinking to the ground to lie face downward.

Collins grabbed him by the shoulder. "Here it is. Here's your drink. Turn over, man. Turn over for your own sake!"

With Collins hauling at his shoulder, the officer twisted his body. There was the faintest shadow of a smile on his lips as he looked at Collins. He gave a sigh like the sigh of a little child.

Collins tried to hold the bucket steadily, but his shaking hands made the water splash all over the face of the dying man. Then he jerked it away and ran on.

The regiment gave him a welcoming roar. The dirty faces were wrinkled in laughter.

His captain waved the bucket away. "Give it to the men."

The two happy-go-lucky lieutenants were the first to get hold of it. They played over it in their fashion.

When one tried to drink, the other teasingly knocked his elbow. "Don't, Billie! You'll make me spill it," said the one. The other laughed.

Suddenly there was a curse, the thud of wood on the ground, and a swift murmur of surprise among the soldiers. The lieutenants glared at each other. The bucket lay on the ground, empty.

Beware
of the Dog

# Beware of the Dog

**Roald Dahl**

*Second World War*

Down below there was only a vast white undulating sea of cloud. Above there was the sun, and the sun was white like the clouds, because it is never yellow when one looks at it from high in the air.

He was still flying the Spitfire. His right hand was on the stick, and he was working the rudder bar with his left leg alone. It was quite easy. The machine was flying well, and he knew what he was doing.

Everything is fine, he thought. I'm doing all right. I'm doing nicely. I know my way home. I'll be there in half an hour. When I land I shall taxi in and switch off my engine and I shall say, help me to get out, will you. I shall make my voice sound ordinary and natural and none of them will take any notice. Then I shall say, someone help me to get out. I can't do it alone because I've lost one of my legs. They'll all laugh and think that I'm joking, and I shall say, all right, come and have a look. Then Yorky will climb up onto the wing and look inside. He'll probably be sick because of all the blood and the mess. I shall laugh and say, for Heaven's sake, help me out.

He glanced down again at his right leg. There was not much of it left. The cannon shell had taken him on the thigh, just above the knee, and now there was nothing but a great mess and a lot of blood. But there was no pain. When he looked down, he felt as though he were seeing something that did not belong to him. It had nothing to do with him. It was just a mess which happened to be there in the cockpit – something strange and unusual and rather interesting. It was like finding a dead cat on the sofa.

He really felt fine, and because he still felt fine, he felt excited and unafraid.

I won't even bother to call up on the radio for the blood wagon, he thought. It isn't necessary. And when I land I'll sit there quite normally and say, some of you fellows come and help me out, will you, because I've lost one of my legs. That will be funny. I'll laugh a little while I'm saying it, I'll say it calmly and slowly, and they'll think I'm joking. When Yorky comes up onto

the wing and gets sick, I'll say, Yorky, have you fixed my car yet?
Then when I get out I'll make my report and later I'll go up to
London. I won't say much until it's time to go to bed, then I'll
say, Bluey, I've got a surprise for you. I lost a leg today. But I don't
mind so long as you don't. It doesn't even hurt. We'll go everywhere in cars. I always hated walking, except when I walked
down the street of the coppersmiths in Baghdad, but I could go
in a rickshaw. I could go home and chop wood, but the head
always flies off the axe. Hot water, that's what it needs, put it
in the bath and make the handle swell. I chopped lots of wood
last time I went home, and I put the axe in the bath. . . .

Then he saw the sun shining on the engine cowling of his
machine. He saw the rivets in the metal, and he remembered
where he was. He realised that he was no longer feeling good;
that he was sick and giddy. His head kept falling forward onto his
chest because his neck seemed no longer to have any strength.
But he knew that he was flying the Spitfire, and he could feel the
handle of the stick between the fingers of his right hand.

I'm going to pass out, he thought. Any moment now I'm
going to pass out.

He looked at his altimeter. Twenty-one thousand. To test
himself he tried to read the hundreds as well as the thousands.
Twenty-one thousand and what? As he looked the dial became
blurred, and he could not even see the needle. He knew then
that he must bail out; that there was not a second to lose, otherwise he would become unconscious. Quickly, frantically, he
tried to slide back the hood with his left hand, but he had not
the strength. For a second he took his right hand off the stick,
and with both hands he managed to push the hood back. The
rush of cold air on his face seemed to help. He had a moment of
great clearness, and his actions became orderly and precise.
That is what happens with a good pilot. He took some quick
deep breaths from his oxygen mask, and as he did so, he looked
out over the side of the cockpit. Down below there was only a
vast white sea of cloud, and he realized that he did not know
where he was.

It'll be the Channel, he thought. I'm sure to fall in the drink.

He throttled back, pulled off his helmet, undid his straps, and
pushed the stick hard over to the left. The Spitfire dipped its
port wing, and turned smoothly over onto its back. The pilot
fell out.

As he fell he opened his eyes, because he knew that he must

not pass out before he had pulled the cord. On one side he saw the sun; on the other he saw the whiteness of the clouds, and as he fell, as he somersaulted in the air, the white clouds chased the sun and the sun chased the clouds. They chased each other in a small circle; they ran faster and faster, and there was the sun and the clouds and the clouds and the sun, and the clouds came nearer until suddenly there was no longer any sun, but only a great whiteness. The whole world was white, and there was nothing in it. It was so white that sometimes it looked black, and after a time it was either white or black, but mostly it was white. He watched it as it turned from white to black, and then back to white again, and the white stayed for a long time, but the black lasted only for a few seconds. He got into the habit of going to sleep during the white periods, and of waking up just in time to see the world when it was black. But the black was very quick. Sometimes it was only a flash, like someone switching off the light, and switching it on again at once, and so whenever it was white, he dozed off.

One day, when it was white, he put out a hand and he touched something. He took it between his fingers and crumpled it. For a time he lay there, idly letting the tips of his fingers play with the thing which they had touched. Then slowly he opened his eyes, looked down at his hand, and saw that he was holding something which was white. It was the edge of a sheet. He knew it was a sheet because he could see the texture of the material and the stitchings on the hem. He screwed up his eyes, and opened them again quickly. This time he saw the room. He saw the bed in which he was lying; he saw the grey walls and the door and the green curtains over the window. There were some roses on the table by his bed.

Then he saw the basin on the table near the roses. It was a white enamel basin, and beside it there was a small medicine glass.

This is a hospital, he thought. I am in a hospital. But he could remember nothing. He lay back on his pillow, looking at the ceiling and wondering what had happened. He was gazing at the smooth greyness of the ceiling which was so clean and grey, and then suddenly he saw a fly walking upon it. The sight of this fly, the suddenness of seeing this small black speck on a sea of grey, brushed the surface of his brain, and quickly, in that second, he remembered everything. He remembered the Spitfire and he remembered the altimeter showing twenty-one thousand feet. He remembered the pushing back of the hood with both hands, and he remembered the bailing out. He remembered his leg.

It seemed all right now. He looked down at the end of the bed, but he could not tell. He put one hand underneath the bedclothes and felt for his knees. He found one of them, but when he felt for the other, his hand touched something which was soft and covered in bandages.

Just then the door opened and a nurse came in.

"Hello," she said. "So you've woken up at last."

She was not good-looking, but she was large and clean. She was between thirty and forty and she had fair hair. More than that he did not notice.

"Where am I?"

"You're a lucky fellow. You landed in a wood near the beach. You're in Brighton. They brought you in two days ago, and now you're all fixed up. You look fine."

"I've lost a leg," he said.

"That's nothing. We'll get you another one. Now you must go to sleep. The doctor will be coming to see you in about an hour." She picked up the basin and the medicine glass and went out.

But he did not sleep. He wanted to keep his eyes open because he was frightened that if he shut them again everything would go away. He lay looking at the ceiling. The fly was still there. It was very energetic. It would run forward very fast for a few inches, then it would stop. Then it would run forward again, stop, run forward, stop, and every now and then it would take off and buzz around viciously in small circles. It always landed back in the same place on the ceiling and started running and stopping all over again. He watched it for so long that after awhile it was no longer a fly, but only a black speck upon a sea of grey, and he was still watching it when the nurse opened the door, and stood aside while the doctor came in. He was an Army doctor, a major, and he had some last war ribbons on his chest. He was bald and small, but he had a cheerful face and kind eyes.

"Well, well," he said. "So you've decided to wake up at last. How are you feeling?"

"I feel all right."

"That's the stuff. You'll be up and about in no time."

The doctor took his wrist to feel his pulse.

"By the way," he said, "some of the lads from your squadron

were ringing up and asking about you. They wanted to come along and see you, but I said that they'd better wait a day or two. Told them you were all right, and that they could come and see you a little later on. Just lie quiet and take it easy for a bit. Got something to read?" He glanced at the table with the roses. "No. Well, nurse will look after you. She'll get you anything you want." With that he waved his hand and went out, followed by the large clean nurse.

When they had gone, he lay back and looked at the ceiling again. The fly was still there and as he lay watching it he heard the noise of an aeroplane in the distance. He lay listening to the sound of its engines. It was a long way away. I wonder what it is, he thought. Let me see if I can place it. Suddenly he jerked his head sharply to one side. Anyone who has been bombed can tell the noise of a Junkers 88. They can tell most other German bombers for that matter, but especially a Junkers 88. The engines seem to sing a duet. There is a deep vibrating bass voice and with it there is a high-pitched tenor. It is the singing of the tenor which makes the sound of a JU-88 something which one cannot mistake.

He lay listening to the noise, and he felt quite certain about what it was. But where were the sirens, and where the guns? That German pilot had a nerve coming near Brighton alone in daylight.

The aircraft was always far away and soon the noise faded away into the distance. Later on there was another. This one, too, was far away but there was the same deep undulating bass and the high singing tenor, and there was no mistaking it. He had heard that noise every day during the battle.

He was puzzled. There was a bell on the table by the bed. He reached out his hand and rang it. He heard the noise of footsteps down the corridor, and the nurse came in.

"Nurse, what were those aeroplanes?"

"I'm sure I don't know. I didn't hear them. Probably fighters or bombers. I expect they were returning from France. Why, what's the matter?"

"They were JU-88s. I'm sure they were JU-88s. I know the sound of the engines. There were two of them. What were they doing over here?"

The nurse came up to the side of his bed and began to straighten the sheets and tuck them in under the mattress.

"Gracious me, what things you imagine. You mustn't worry

about a thing like that. Would you like me to get you something to read?"

"No, thank you."

She patted his pillow and brushed back the hair from his forehead with her hand.

"They never come over in daylight any longer. You know that. They were probably Lancasters or Flying Fortresses."

"Nurse."

"Yes."

"Could I have a cigarette?"

"Why certainly you can."

She went out and came back almost at once with a packet of Players and some matches. She handed one to him and when he had put it in his mouth, she struck a match and lit it.

"If you want me again," she said, "just ring the bell," and she went out.

Once toward evening he heard the noise of another aircraft. It was far away, but even so he knew that it was a single-engined machine. But he could not place it. It was going fast; he could tell that. But it wasn't a Spit, and it wasn't a Hurricane. It did not sound like an American engine either. They make more noise. He did not know what it was, and it worried him greatly. Perhaps I am very ill, he thought. Perhaps I am imagining things. Perhaps I am a little delirious. I simply do not know what to think.

That evening the nurse came in with a basin of hot water and began to wash him.

"Well," she said, "I hope you don't still think that we're being bombed."

She had taken off his pyjama top and was soaping his right arm with a flannel. He did not answer.

She rinsed the flannel in the water, rubbed more soap on it, and began to wash his chest.

"You're looking fine this evening," she said. "They operated on you as soon as you came in. They did a marvellous job. You'll be all right. I've got a brother in the RAF," she added. "Flying bombers."

He said, "I went to school in Brighton."

She looked up quickly. "Well, that's fine," she said. "I expect you'll know some people in the town."

"Yes," he said, "I know quite a few."

She had finished washing his chest and arms, and now she

turned back the bedclothes, so that his left leg was uncovered. She did it in such a way that his bandaged stump remained under the sheets. She undid the cord of his pyjama trousers and took them off. There was no trouble because they had cut off the right trouser leg, so that it could not interfere with the bandages. She began to wash his left leg and the rest of his body. This was the first time he had had a bed bath, and he was embarrassed. She laid a towel under his leg, and she was washing his foot with the flannel. She said, "This wretched soap won't lather at all. It's the water. It's as hard as nails."

He said, "None of the soap is very good now and, of course, with hard water it's hopeless." As he said it he remembered something. He remembered the baths which he used to take at school in Brighton, in the long stone-floored bathroom which had four baths in a room. He remembered how the water was so soft that you had to take a shower afterwards to get all the soap off your body, and he remembered how the foam used to float on the surface of the water, so that you could not see your legs underneath. He remembered that sometimes they were given calcium tablets because the school doctor used to say that soft water was bad for the teeth.

"In Brighton," he said, "the water isn't . . . "

He did not finish the sentence. Something had occurred to him; something so fantastic and absurd that for a moment he felt like telling the nurse about it and having a good laugh.

She looked up. "The water isn't what?" she said.

"Nothing," he answered. "I was dreaming."

She rinsed the flannel in the basin, wiped the soap off his leg, and dried him with a towel.

"It's nice to be washed," he said. "I feel better." He was feeling his face with his hands. "I need a shave."

"We'll do that tomorrow," she said. "Perhaps you can do it yourself then."

That night he could not sleep. He lay awake thinking of the Junkers 88s and of the hardness of the water. He could think of nothing else. They were JU-88s, he said to himself. I know they were. And yet it is not possible, because they would not be flying so low over here in broad daylight. I know that it is true, and yet I know that it is impossible. Perhaps I am ill. Perhaps I am behaving like a fool and do not know what I am doing or saying. Perhaps I am delirious. For a long time he lay awake thinking these things, and once he sat up in bed and said aloud,

"I will prove that I am not crazy. I will make a little speech about something complicated and intellectual. I will talk about what to do with Germany after the war." But before he had time to begin, he was asleep.

He woke just as the first light of day was showing through the slit in the curtains over the window. The room was still dark, but he could tell that it was already beginning to get light outside. He lay looking at the grey light which was showing through the slit in the curtain, and as he lay there he remembered the day before. He remembered the Junkers 88s and the hardness of the water; he remembered the large pleasant nurse and the kind doctor, and now the small grain of doubt took root in his mind and it began to grow.

He looked around the room. The nurse had taken the roses out the night before, and there was nothing except the table with a packet of cigarettes, a box of matches, and an ash tray. Otherwise, it was bare. It was no longer warm or friendly. It was not even comfortable. It was cold and empty and very quiet.

Slowly the grain of doubt grew, and with it came fear, a light, dancing fear that warned but did not frighten; the kind of fear that one gets not because one is afraid, but because one feels that there is something wrong. Quickly the doubt and the fear grew so that he became restless and angry, and when he touched his forehead with his hand, he found that it was damp with sweat. He knew then that he must do something; that he must find some way of proving to himself that he was either right or wrong, and he looked up and saw again the window and the green curtains. From where he lay, that window was right in front of him, but it was fully ten yards away. Somehow he must reach it and look out. The idea became an obsession with him, and soon he could think of nothing except the window. But what about his leg? He put his hand underneath the bedclothes and felt the thick bandaged stump which was all that was left on the right-hand side. It seemed all right. It didn't hurt. But it would not be easy.

He sat up. Then he pushed the bedclothes aside and put his left leg on the floor. Slowly, carefully, he swung his body over until he had both hands on the floor as well; and then he was out of bed, kneeling on the carpet. He looked at the stump. It was very short and thick, covered with bandages. It was beginning to hurt and he could feel it throbbing. He wanted to collapse, lie down on the carpet and do nothing, but he knew that he must go on.

With two arms and one leg, he crawled over towards the window. He would reach forward as far as he could with his arms, then he would give a little jump and slide his left leg along after them. Each time he did, it jarred his wound so that he gave a soft grunt of pain, but he continued to crawl across the floor on two hands and one knee. When he got to the window he reached up, and one at a time he placed both hands on the sill. Slowly he raised himself up until he was standing on his left leg. Then quickly he pushed aside the curtains and looked out.

He saw a small house with a grey tiled roof standing alone beside a narrow lane, and immediately behind it there was a ploughed field. In front of the house there was an untidy garden, and there was a green hedge separating the garden from the lane. He was looking at the hedge when he saw the sign. It was just a piece of board nailed to the top of a short pole, and because the hedge had not been trimmed for a long time, the branches had grown out around the sign so that it seemed almost as though it had been placed in the middle of the hedge. There was something written on the board with white paint, and he pressed his head against the glass of the window, trying to read what it said. The first letter was a G, he could see that. The second was an A, and the third was an R. One after another he managed to see what the letters were. There were three words, and slowly he spelled the letters out loud to himself as he managed to read them. G-A-R-D-E A-U C-H-I-E-N. *Garde au chien.*[1] That is what it said.

He stood there balancing on one leg and holding tightly to the edges of the window sill with his hands, staring at the sign and at the whitewashed lettering of the words. For a moment he could think of nothing at all. He stood there looking at the sign, repeating the words over and over to himself, and then slowly he began to realise the full meaning of the thing. He looked up at the cottage and at the ploughed field. He looked at the small orchard on the left of the cottage and he looked at the countryside beyond. "So this is France," he said. "I am in France."

Now the throbbing in his right thigh was very great. It felt as though someone was pounding the end of the stump with a hammer, and suddenly the pain became so intense that it affected his head and for a moment he thought he was going to fall. Quickly he knelt down again, crawled back to the bed

[1] Beware of the dog

and hoisted himself in. He pulled the bedclothes over himself and lay back on the pillow exhausted. He could still think of nothing at all except the small sign by the hedges, and the ploughed field and the orchard. It was the words on the sign that he could not forget.

It was some time before the nurse came in. She came carrying a basin of hot water and she said, "Good morning, how are you today?"

He said, "Good morning, nurse."

The pain was still great under the bandages, but he did not wish to tell this woman anything. He looked at her as she busied herself with getting the washing things ready. He looked at her more carefully now. Her hair was very fair. She was tall and big-boned, and her face seemed pleasant. But there was something a little uneasy about her eyes. They were never still. They never looked at anything for more than a moment and they moved too quickly from one place to another in the room. There was something about her movements also. They were too sharp and nervous to go well with the casual manner in which she spoke.

She set down the basin, took off his pyjama top and began to wash him.

"Did you sleep well?"

"Yes."

"Good," she said. She was washing his arms and his chest.

"I believe there's someone coming down to see you from the Air Ministry after breakfast," she went on. "They want a report or something. I expect you know all about it. How you got shot down and all that. I won't let him stay long, so don't worry."

He did not answer. She finished washing him, and gave him a toothbrush and some tooth powder. He brushed his teeth, rinsed his mouth, and spat the water out into the basin.

Later she brought him his breakfast on a tray, but he did not want to eat. He was still feeling weak and sick, and he wished only to lie still and think about what had happened. And there was a sentence running through his head. It was a sentence which Johnny, the Intelligence Officer of his squadron, always repeated to the pilots every day before they went out. He could see Johnny now, leaning against the wall of the dispersal hut with his pipe in his hand, saying, "And if they get you, don't forget, just your name, rank, and number. Nothing else. For God's sake, say nothing else."

"There you are," she said as she put the tray on his lap. "I've got you an egg. Can you manage all right?"

"Yes."

She stood beside the bed. "Are you feeling all right?"

"Yes."

"Good. If you want another egg I might be able to get you one."

"This is all right."

"Well, just ring the bell if you want any more." And she went out.

He had just finished eating, when the nurse came in again.

She said, "Wing Commander Roberts is here. I've told him that he can only stay for a few minutes."

She beckoned with her hand and the Wing Commander came in.

"Sorry to bother you like this," he said.

He was an ordinary RAF officer, dressed in a uniform which was a little shabby, and he wore wings and a DFC. He was fairly tall and thin with plenty of black hair. His teeth, which were irregular and widely spaced, stuck out a little even when he closed his mouth. As he spoke he took a printed form and a pencil from his pocket, and he pulled up a chair and sat down.

"How are you feeling?"

There was no answer.

"Tough luck about your leg. I know how you feel. I hear you put up a fine show before they got you."

The man in the bed was lying quite still, watching the man in the chair.

The man in the chair said, "Well, let's get this stuff over. I'm afraid you'll have to answer a few questions so that I can fill in this combat report. Let me see now, first of all, what was your squadron?"

The man in the bed did not move. He looked straight at the Wing Commander and he said, "My name is Peter Williamson. My rank is Squadron Leader and my number is nine seven two four five seven."

# Shall Not Perish

# Shall Not Perish

**William Faulkner**

*Second World War*

When the message came about Pete, Father and I had already
gone to the field. Mother got it out of the mailbox after we left
and brought it down to the fence, and she already knew before-
hand what it was because she didn't even have on her sun-
bonnet, so she must have been watching from the kitchen
window when the carrier drove up. And I already knew what
was in it too. Because she didn't speak. She just stood at the
fence with the little pale envelope that didn't even need a
stamp on it in her hand, and it was me that hollered at Father,
from further away across the field than he was, so that he
reached the fence first where Mother waited even though I was
already running. "I know what it is," Mother said. "But I
can't open it. Open it."

"No it ain't!" I hollered, running. "No it ain't!" Then I
was hollering, "No, Pete! No, Pete!" Then I was hollering,
"God damn them Japs! God damn them Japs!" and then I
was the one Father had to grab and hold, trying to hold me,
having to wrastle with me like I was another man instead of
just nine.

And that was all. One day there was Pearl Harbor. And the
next week Pete went to Memphis, to join the army and go there
and help them; and one morning Mother stood at the field
fence with a little scrap of paper not even big enough to start
a fire with, that didn't even need a stamp on the envelope,
saying, *A ship was. Now it is not. Your son was one of them.* And we
allowed ourselves one day to grieve, and that was all. Because
it was April, the hardest middle push of planting time, and
there was the land, the seventy acres which were our bread and
fire and keep, which had outlasted the Griers before us because
they had done right by it, and had outlasted Pete because while
he was here he had done his part to help and would outlast
Mother and Father and me if we did ours.

Then it happened again. Maybe we had forgotten that it
could and was going to, again and again, to people who loved

sons and brothers as we loved Pete, until the day finally came when there would be an end to it. After that day when we saw Pete's name and picture in the Memphis paper, Father would bring one home with him each time he went to town. And we would see the pictures and names of soldiers and sailors from other counties and towns in Mississippi and Arkansas and Tennessee, but there wasn't another from ours, and so after a while it did look like Pete was going to be all.

Then it happened again. It was late July, a Friday. Father had gone to town early on Homer Bookwright's cattletruck and now it was sundown. I had just come up from the field with the light sweep and I had just finished stalling the mule and come out of the barn when Homer's truck stopped at the mailbox and Father got down and came up the lane, with a sack of flour balanced on his shoulder and a package under his arm and the folded newspaper in his hand. And I took one look at the folded paper and then no more. Because I knew it too, even if he always did have one when he came back from town. Because it was bound to happen sooner or later; it would not be just us out of all Yoknapatawpha County who had loved enough to have sole right to grief. So I just met him and took part of the load and turned beside him, and we entered the kitchen together where our cold supper waited on the table and Mother sat in the last of sunset in the open door, her hand and arm strong and steady on the dasher of the churn.

When the message came about Pete, Father never touched her. He didn't touch her now. He just lowered the flour onto the table and went to the chair and held out the folded paper. "It's Major de Spain's boy," he said. "In town. The av-aytor. That was home last fall in his officer uniform. He run his airplane into a Japanese battleship and blowed it up. So they knowed where he was at." And Mother didn't stop the churn for a minute either, because even I could tell that the butter had almost come. Then she got up and went to the sink and washed her hands and came back and sat down again.

"Read it," she said.

So Father and I found out that Mother not only knew all the time it was going to happen again, but that she already knew what she was going to do when it did, not only this time but the next one too, and the one after that and the one after that, until the day finally came when all the grieving about the earth, the rich and the poor too, whether they lived with ten nigger servants in the fine big painted houses in town or whether they lived on and by seventy acres of not extra good land like us or whether all they owned was the right to sweat today for what they would eat tonight, could say, *At least this there was some point to why we grieved.*

We fed and milked and came back and ate the cold supper, and I built a fire in the stove and Mother put on the kettle and whatever else would heat enough water for two, and I fetched in the washtub from the back porch, and while Mother washed the dishes and cleaned up the kitchen, Father and I sat on the front steps. This was about the time of day that Pete and I would walk the two miles down to Old Man Killegrew's house last December, to listen to the radio tell about Pearl Harbor and Manila. But more than Pearl Harbor and Manila has happened since then, and Pete don't make one to listen to it. Nor do I: it's like, since nobody can tell us exactly where he was when he stopped being *is*, instead of just becoming *was* at some single spot on the earth where the people who loved him could weight him down with a stone, Pete still *is* everywhere about the earth, one among all the fighters forever, *was* or *is* either. So Mother and Father and I don't need a little wooden box to catch the voices of them that saw the courage and the sacrifice. Then Mother called me back to the kitchen. The water smoked a little in the washtub, beside the soap dish and my clean nightshirt and the towel Mother made out of our worn-out cotton sacks, and I bathe and empty the tub and leave it ready for her, and we lie down.

Then morning, and we rose. Mother was up first, as always. My clean white Sunday shirt and pants were waiting, along with the shoes and stockings I hadn't even seen since frost was out of the ground. But in yesterday's overalls still I carried the shoes back to the kitchen where Mother stood in yesterday's dress at the stove where not only our breakfast was cooking but Father's dinner too, and set the shoes beside her Sunday ones against the wall and went to the barn, and Father and I fed and milked and came back and sat down and ate while Mother moved back and forth between the table and the stove till we were done, and she herself sat down. Then I got out the blacking-box, until Father came and took it away from me – the polish and rag and brush and the four shoes in succession. "De Spain is rich," he said. "With a monkey nigger in a white coat to hold the jar up each time he wants to spit. You shine all shoes like you aimed yourself to wear them: just the parts that you can see yourself by looking down."

Then we dressed. I put on my Sunday shirt and the pants so stiff with starch that they would stand alone, and carried my stockings back to the kitchen just as Mother entered, carrying hers, and dressed too, even her hat, and took my stockings from me and put them with hers on the table beside the shined shoes, and lifted the satchel down from the cupboard shelf. It was still in the cardboard box it came in, with the colored label of the San Francisco drugstore where Pete bought it – a round, square-ended, water-proof satchel with a handle for carrying, so that as soon as Pete saw it in the store he must have known too that it had been almost exactly made for exactly what we would use it for, with a zipper opening that Mother had never seen before nor Father either. That is, we had all three been in the drugstore and the ten-cent-store in Jefferson but I was the only one who had been curious enough to find out how one worked, even though even I never dreamed we would ever own one. So it was me that zipped it open, with a pipe and a can of tobacco in it for Father and a hunting cap with a carbide headlight for me and for Mother the satchel itself, and she zipped it shut and then open and then Father tried it, running the slide up and down the little clicking track until Mother made him stop before he wore it out; and she put the satchel, still open, back into the box and I fetched in from the barn the empty quart bottle of cattle-dip and she scalded the bottle and cork and put them and the clean folded towel into the satchel and set the box onto the cupboard shelf, the zipper still open because when we came to need it we would have to open it first and so we would save that much wear on the zipper too. She took the satchel from the box and the bottle from the satchel and filled the bottle with clean water and corked it and put it back into the satchel with the clean towel and put our shoes and stockings in and zipped the satchel shut, and we walked to the road and stood in the bright hot morning beside the mailbox until the bus came up and stopped.

It was the school bus, the one I rode back and forth to French-man's Bend to school in last winter, and that Pete rode in every morning and evening until he graduated, but going in the opposite direction now, in to Jefferson, and only on Saturday, seen for a long time down the long straight stretch of Valley road while other people waiting beside other mail-boxes got into it. Then it was our turn. Mother handed the two quarters to Solon Quick, who built it and owned it and drove it, and we got in too and it went on, and soon there was no more room for the ones that stood beside the mailboxes and signalled and then it went fast, twenty miles then ten then five then one, and up the last hill to where the concrete streets began, and we got out and sat on the curb and Mother opened the satchel and took our shoes and the bottle of water and the towel and we washed our feet and put on our shoes and stockings and Mother put the bottle and towel back and shut the bag.

And we walked beside the iron picket fence long enough to front a cotton patch; we turned into the yard which was bigger than farms I had seen and followed the gravel drive wider and smoother than roads in Frenchman's Bend, on to the house that to me anyway looked bigger than the court-house, and mounted the steps between the stone columns and crossed the portico that would have held our whole house, galleries and all, and knocked at the door. And then it never mattered whether our shoes were shined at all or not: the whites of the monkey nigger's eyes for just a second when he opened the door for us, the white of his coat for just a second at the end of the hall before it was gone too, his feet not making any more noise than a cat's leaving us to find the right door by ourselves, if we could. And we did – the rich man's parlour that any woman in Frenchman's Bend and I reckon in the rest of the county too could have described to the inch but which not even the men who would come to Major de Spain after bank-hours or on Sunday to ask to have a note extended, had ever seen, with a light hanging in the middle of the ceiling the size of our whole washtub full of chopped-up ice and a gold-coloured harp that would have blocked our barn door and a mirror that a man on a mule could have seen himself and the mule both in, and a table shaped like a coffin in the middle of the floor with the Confederate flag spread over it and the photograph of Major de Spain's son and the open box with the medal in it and a big blue automatic pistol weighting down the flag, and Major de Spain standing at the end of the table with his hat on until after a while he seemed to hear and recognise the name which Mother spoke; – not a real major but just called that because his father had been a real one in the old Confederate war, but a banker powerful in money and politics both, that Father said had made governors and senators too in Mississippi; – an old man, too old you would have said to have had a son just twenty-three; too old anyway to have had that look on his face.

"Ha," he said. "I remember now. You too were advised that your son poured out his blood on the altar of unpreparedness and inefficiency. What do you want?"

"Nothing," Mother said. She didn't even pause at the door. She went on toward the table. "We had nothing to bring you. And I don't think I see anything here we would want to take away."

"You're wrong," he said. "You have a son left. Take what they have been advising to me: go back home and pray. Not for the dead one: for the one they have so far left you, that something somewhere, somehow will save him!" She wasn't even looking at him. She never had looked at him again. She just went on across that barn-sized room exactly as I have watched her set mine and Father's lunch pail into the fence corner when there wasn't time to stop the plough to eat, and turn back toward the house.

"I can tell you something simpler than that," she said. "Weep." Then she reached the table. But it was only her body that stopped, her hand going out so smooth and quick that his hand only caught her wrist, the two hands locked together on the big blue pistol, between the photograph and the little hunk of iron medal on its coloured ribbon, against that old flag that a heap of people I knew had never seen and a heap more of them wouldn't recognise if they did, and over all of it the old man's voice that ought not to have sounded like that either.

"For his country! He had no country: this one I too repudiate. His country and mine both was ravaged and polluted and destroyed eighty years ago, before even I was born. His forefathers fought and died for it then, even though what they fought and lost for was a dream. He didn't even have a dream. He died for an illusion. In the interests of usury,[1] by the folly and rapacity of politicians, for the glory and aggrandisement of organised labour!"

"Yes," Mother said. "Weep."

"The fear of elective servants for their incumbencies! The subservience of misled workingmen for the demagogues who misled them! Shame? Grief? How can poltroonery and rapacity and voluntary thralldom know shame or grief?"

"All men are capable of shame," Mother said. "Just as all

[1] the lending of money for interest

73

men are capable of courage and honour and sacrifice. And grief too. It will take time, but they will learn it. It will take more grief than yours and mine, and there will be more. But it will be enough."

"When? When all the young men are dead? What will there be left then worth the saving?"

"I know," Mother said. "I know. Our Pete was too young too to have to die." Then I realised that their hands were no longer locked, that he was erect again and that the pistol was hanging slack in Mother's hand against her side, and for a minute I thought she was going to unzip the satchel and take the towel out of it. But she just laid the pistol back on the table and stepped up to him and took the handkerchief from his breast pocket and put it into his hand and stepped back. "That's right." she said. "Weep. Not for him: for us, the old, who don't know why. What is your Negro's name?"

But he didn't answer. He didn't even raise the handkerchief to his face. He just stood there holding it, like he hadn't discovered yet that it was in his hand, or perhaps even what it was Mother had put there. "For us, the old," he said. "You believe. You have had three months to learn again, to find out why; mine happened yesterday. Tell me."

"I don't know," Mother said. "Maybe women are not supposed to know why their sons must die in battle; maybe all they are supposed to do is just grieve for them. But my son knew why. And my brother went to the war when I was a girl, and our mother didn't know why either, but he did. And my grandfather was in that old one there too, and I reckon his mother didn't know why either, but I reckon he did. And my son knew why he had to go to this one, and he knew I knew he did even though I didn't, just as he knew that this child here and I both knew he would not come back. But he knew why, even if I didn't, couldn't, never can. So it must be all right, even if I couldn't understand it. Because there is nothing in him that I or his father didn't put there. What is your Negro's name?"

He called the name then. And the nigger wasn't so far away after all, though when he entered Major de Spain had already turned so that his back was toward the door. He didn't look around. He just pointed toward the table with the hand Mother had put the handkerchief into, and the nigger went to the table without looking at anybody and without making any more noise on the floor than a cat and he didn't stop at all; it looked to me like he had already turned and started back before he even reached the table: one flick of the black hand and the white sleeve and the pistol vanished without me even seeing him touch it and when he passed me again going out, I couldn't see what he had done with it. So Mother had to speak twice before I knew she was talking to me.

"Come," she said.

"Wait," said Major de Spain. He had turned again, facing us. "What you and his father gave him. You must know what that was."

"I know it came a long way," Mother said. "So it must have been strong to have lasted through all of us. It must have been all right for him to be willing to die for it after that long time and coming that far. Come," she said again.

"Wait," he said. "Wait. Where did you come from?"

Mother stopped. "I told you: Frenchman's Bend."

"I know. How? By wagon? You have no car."

"Oh," Mother said. "We came in Mr Quick's bus. He comes in every Saturday."

"And waits until night to go back. I'll send you back in my car." He called the nigger's name again. But Mother stopped him. "Thank you," she said. "We have already paid Mr Quick. He owes us the ride back home."

There was an old lady born and raised in Jefferson who died rich somewhere in the North and left some money to the town to build a museum with. It was a house like a church, built for nothing else except to hold the pictures she picked out to put in it – pictures from all over the United States, painted by people who loved what they had seen or where they had been born or lived enough to want to paint pictures of it so that other people could see it too; pictures of men and women and children, and the houses and streets and cities and the woods and fields and streams where they worked or lived or pleasured, so that all the people who wanted to, people like us from Frenchman's Bend of from littler places even than Frenchman's Bend in our county or beyond our state too, could come without charge into the cool and the quiet and look without let at the pictures of men and women and children who were the same people that we were even if their houses and barns were different and their fields worked different, with different things growing in them. So it was already late when we left the museum, and later still when we got back to where the bus waited, and later still more before we got started, although at least we could get into the bus and take our shoes and stockings back off. Because Mrs Quick hadn't come yet and so Solon had to wait for her, not because she was his wife but because he made her pay a quarter out of her egg-money to ride to town and back on Saturday, and he wouldn't go off and leave anybody who had paid him. And so, even though the bus ran fast again, when the road finally straightened out into the long Valley stretch, there was only the last sunset spoking out across the sky, stretching all the way across America from the Pacific ocean, touching all the places that the men and women in the museum whose names we didn't even know had loved enough to paint pictures of them, like a big soft fading wheel.

And I remembered how Father used to always prove any point he wanted to make to Pete and me, by Grandfather. It didn't matter whether it was something he thought we ought to have done and hadn't, or something he would have stopped us from doing if he had just known about it in time. "Now, take your Grandpap," he would say. I could remember him too: Father's grandfather even, old, so old you just wouldn't believe it, so old that it would seem to me he must have gone clean back to the old fathers in Genesis and Exodus that talked face to face with God, and Grandpap outlived them all except him. It seemed to me he must have been too old even to have actually fought in the old Confederate war, although that was about all he talked about, not only when we thought that maybe he was awake but even when we knew he must be asleep, until after a while we had to admit that we never knew which one he really was. He would sit in his chair under the mulberry in the yard or on the sunny end of the front gallery or in his corner by the hearth; he would start up out of the chair and we still wouldn't know which one he was, whether he never had been asleep or whether he hadn't ever waked even when he jumped up, hollering, "Look out! Look out! Here they come!" He wouldn't even always holler the same name; they wouldn't even always be on the same side or even soldiers: Forrest, or Morgan, or Abe Lincoln, or Van Dorn, or Grant or Colonel Sartoris himself, whose people still lived in our country, or Mrs Rosa Millard, Colonel Sartoris's mother-in-law who stood off the Yankees and carpetbaggers[1] too for the whole four years of the war until

---

[1] Northerners who went south seeking private gain or political advancement

Colonel Sartoris could get back home. Pete thought it was just funny. Father and I were ashamed. We didn't know what Mother thought nor even what it was, until the afternoon at the picture show.

It was a continued picture, a Western; it seemed to me that it had been running every Saturday afternoon for years. Pete and Father and I would go in to town every Saturday to see it, and sometimes Mother would go too, to sit there in the dark while the pistols popped and snapped and the horses galloped and each time it would look like they were going to catch him but you knew they wouldn't quite, that there would be some more of it next Saturday and the one after that and the one after that, and always the week in between for me and Pete to talk about the villain's pearl-handled pistol that Pete wished was his and the hero's spotted horse that I wished was mine. Then one Saturday Mother decided to take Grandpap. He sat between her and me, already asleep again, so old now that he didn't even have to snore, until the time came that you could have set a watch by every Saturday afternoon: when the horses all came plunging down the cliff and whirled around and came boiling up the gully until in just one more jump they would come clean out of the screen and go galloping among the little faces turned up to them like corn shucks scattered across a lot. Then Grandpap waked up. For about five seconds he sat perfectly still. I could even feel him sitting still, he sat so still so hard. Then he said, "Cavalry!" Then he was on his feet. "Forrest!" he said. "Bedford Forrest! Get out of here! Get out of the way!" clawing and scrabbling from one seat to the next one whether there was anybody in them or not, into the aisle with us trying to follow and catch him and up the aisle toward the door still hollering, "Forrest! Forrest! Here he comes! Get out of the way!" and outside at last, with half the show behind us and Grandpap blinking and trembling at the light and Pete propped against the wall by his arms like he was being sick, laughing, and father shaking Grandpap's arm and saying, "You old fool! You old fool!" until Mother made him stop. And we half carried him around to the alley where the wagon was hitched and helped him in and Mother got in and sat by him, holding his hand until he could begin to stop shaking. "Go get him a bottle of beer," she said.

"He don't deserve any beer," Father said. "The old fool, having the whole town laughing . . . ."

"Go get him some beer!" Mother said. "He's going to sit right here in his own wagon and drink it. Go on!" And Father did, and Mother held the bottle until Grandpap got a good hold on it, and she sat holding his hand until he got a good swallow down him. Then he begun to stop shaking. He said, "Ah-h-h," and took another swallow and said, "Ah-h-h," again and then he even drew his other hand out of Mother's and he wasn't trembling now but just a little, taking little darting sips at the bottle and saying "Hah!" and taking another sip and saying "Hah!" again, and not just looking at the bottle now but looking all around, and his eyes snapping a little when he blinked. "Fools yourselves!" Mother cried at Father and Pete and me. "He wasn't running from anybody! He was running in front of them, hollering at all clods to look out because better men than they were coming, even seventy-five years afterwards, still powerful, still dangerous, still coming!"

And I knew them too. I had seen them too, who had never been further from Frenchman's Bend than I could return by night to sleep. It was like the wheel, like the sunset itself, hubbed at that little place that don't even show on a map, that not two hundred people out of all the earth know is named French-man's Bend or has any name at all, and spoking out in all the directions and touching them all, never a one too big for it to touch, never a one too little to be remembered: – the places that men and women have lived in and loved whether they had anything to paint pictures of them with or not, all the little places quiet enough to be lived in and loved and the names of them before they were quiet enough, and the names of the deeds that made them quiet enough and the names of the men and the women who did the deeds, who lasted and endured and fought the battles and lost them and fought again because they didn't even know they had been whipped, and tamed the wilderness and overpassed the mountains and deserts and died and still went on as the shape of the United States grew and went on. I knew them too: the men and women still powerful seventy-five years and twice that and twice that again after-ward, still powerful and still dangerous and still coming, North and South and East and West, until the name of what they did and what they died for became just one single word, louder than any thunder. It was America, and it covered all the western earth.

# Christmas Truce

# Christmas Truce

**Robert Graves**

*First World War*

Young Stan comes around yesterday about tea-time – you know my grandson Stan? He's a Polytechnic student, just turned twenty, as smart as his dad was at the same age. Stan's all out to be a commercial artist and do them big coloured posters for the hoardings. Doesn't answer to "Stan", though – says it's "common"; says he's either "Stanley", or he's nothing.

Stan's got a bagful of big, noble ideas; all schemed out carefully, with what he calls "captions" attached.

Well, I can't say nothing against big, noble ideas. I was a redhot Labour-man myself for a time, forty years ago now, when the Kayser's war ended and the war-profiteers began treading us ex-heroes into the mud. But that's all over long ago – in fact, Labour's got a damn sight too respectable for my taste! Worse than Tories, most of their leaders is now – especially them that used to be the loudest in rendering "We'll Keep the Red Flag Flying Still". They're all Churchwardens now, or country gents, if they're not in the House of Lords.

Anyhow, yesterday Stan came around, about a big Ban-the-Bomb march all the way across England to Trafalgar Square. And couldn't I persuade a few of my old comrades to form a special squad with a banner marked "First World War Veterans Protest Against the Bomb"? He wanted us to head the parade, ribbons, crutches, wheel-chairs and all.

I put my foot down pretty hard. "No, Mr Stanley," I said politely, "I regret as I can't accept your kind invitation."

"But why?" says he. "You don't want another war, Grandfather, do you? You don't want mankind to be annihilated? This time it won't be just a few unlucky chaps killed, like Uncle Arthur in the First War, and Dad in the Second . . . It will be all mankind."

"Listen, young 'un," I said. "I don't trust nobody who talks about mankind – not parsons, not politicians, nor anyone else. There ain't no such thing as 'mankind', and practically speaking there ain't."

"Practically speaking, Grandfather," says young Stan, "there *is*. Mankind means all the different nations lumped together – us, the Russians, the Americans, the Germans, the French, and all the rest of them. If the bomb goes off, everyone's finished."

"It's not going off," I says.

"But it's gone off twice already – at Hiroshima and Nagasaki," he argues, "so why not again? The damage will be definitely final when it *does* go off."

I wouldn't let Stan have the last word. "In the crazy, old-fashioned war in which I lost my foot," I said, a bit sternly, "the Fritzes used poison gas. They thought it would help 'em to break through at Wipers.[1] But somehow the line held, and soon our factories were churning out the same stinking stuff for us to use to them. All right, and now what about Hitler's war?"

"What about it?" Stan asks.

"Well," I says, "everyone in England was issued an expensive mask in a smart-looking case against poison-gas bombs dropped from the air – me, your Dad, your Ma, and yourself as a tiny tot. But how many poison-gas bombs were dropped on London, or on Berlin? Not a damned one! Both sides were scared stiff. Poison gas had got too deadly. No mask in the market could keep the new sorts out. So there's not going to be no atom bombs dropped neither, I tell you, Stanley my lad; not this side of the Hereafter! Everyone's scared stiff again."

"Then why do both sides manufacture quantities of atom bombs and pile them up?" he asks.

"Search me," I said, "unless it's à clever way of keeping up full employment by making believe there's a war on. What with bombs and fall-out shelters, and radar equipment, and unsinkable aircraft-carriers, and satellites, and shooting rockets at the moon, and keeping up big armies – takes two thousand quid nowadays to maintain a soldier in the field, I read the other day – what with all that play-acting, there's full employment assured for everyone, and businessmen are rubbing their hands."

"Your argument has a bad flaw, Grandfather. The Russians don't need to worry about full employment."

"No," said I, "perhaps they don't. But their politicians and commissars have to keep up the notion of a wicked Capitalist plot to wipe out the poor workers. And they have to show that they're well ahead in the Arms Race. Forget it, lad, forget it!

[1] army slang for Ypres, the site of a major battle in the First World War

Mankind, which is a term used by maiden ladies and bun-punchers, ain't going to be annihilated by no atom bomb."

Stan changed his tactics. "Nevertheless, Grandfather," he says, "we British want to show the Russians that we're not engaged in any such Capitalist plot. All men are brothers, and I for one have nothing against my opposite number in Moscow, Ivan Whoever-he-may-be . . . This protest march is the only, logical way I can show him my dislike of organised propaganda."

"But Ivan Orfalitch ain't here to watch you march; nor the Russian telly ain't going to show him no picture of it. If Ivan thinks you're a bleeding Capitalist, then he'll go on thinking you're a bleeding Capitalist; and he won't be so far out, neither, in my opinion. No, Stan, you can't fight organised propaganda with amachoor propaganda."

"Oh, can it, Grandfather!" says Stan. "You're a professional pessimist. And *you* didn't hate the Germans even when you were fighting them – in spite of the newspapers. What about that Christmas Truce?"

Well, I'd mentioned it to him one day, I own; but it seems he'd drawn the wrong conclusions and didn't want to be put straight. However, I'm a lucky bloke – always being saved by what other blokes call "coincidences," but which I don't; because they always happen when I need 'em most. In the trenches we used to call that "being in God's pocket". So, of course, we hear a knock at the door and a shout, and in steps my old mucking-in chum Dodger Green, formerly 301691, Pte Edward Green of the 1st Batt., North Wessex Regiment – come to town by bus for a Saturday night booze with me, every bit of twenty miles.

"You're here in the exact nick, Dodger," says I, "as once before." He'd nappooed[1] a Fritz officer one day when I was lying with one foot missing outside Delville Wood, and the Fritz was kindly putting us wounded out of our misery with an automatic pistol.

"What's new, Fiddler?" he asks.

"Tell this lad about the *two* Christmas truces," I said. "He's trying to enlist us for a march to Moscow, or somewhere."

"Well," says Dodger, "I don't see no connection, not yet. And marching to Moscow ain't no worse nor marching to Berlin, same as you and me did – and never got more nor a few

[1] killed

hundred yards forward in the three years we were at it. But, all right, I'll give him the facts, since you particularly ask me."

Stan listened quietly while Dodger told his tale. I'd heard it often enough before, but Dodger's yarns improve with the telling. You see, I missed most of that first Christmas Truce, as I'll explain later. But I came in for the second; and saw a part of it what Dodger didn't. And the moral I wanted to impress on young Stan depended on there being *two* truces, not one: them two were a lot different from one another.

I brings a quart bottle of wallop from the kitchen, along with a couple of glasses – not three, because young Stan don't drink anything so "common" as beer – and Dodger held forth. Got a golden tongue, has Dodger – I've seen him hold an audience spellbound at "The Three Feathers" from opening-time to stop-tap, and his glass filled every ten minutes, free.

"Well," he says, "the first truce was in 1914, about four months after the Kayser's war began. They say that the old Pope suggested it, and that the Kayser agreed, but that Joffre, the French C.-in-C. wouldn't allow it. However, the Bavarians were sweating on a short spell of peace and good will, being Catholics, and sent word around that the Pope was going to get his way. Consequently, though we didn't have the Bavarians in front of us, there at Boy Greneer, not a shot was fired on our sector all Christmas Eve. In those days we hadn't been issued with Mills bombs, or trench-mortars, or Verey pistols, or steel helmets, or sand bags, or any of them later luxuries; and only two machine-guns to a battalion. The trenches were shallow and knee-deep in water, so that most of the time we had to crouch on the fire-step. God knows how we kept alive and smiling . . . It wasn't no picnic, was it, Fiddler? – and the ground half-frozen, too!

"Christmas Eve, at 7:30 p.m., the enemy trenches suddenly lit up with a row of coloured Chinese lanterns, and a bonfire started in the village behind. We stood to arms, prepared for whatever happened. Ten minutes later the Fritzes began singing a Christmas carol called 'Stilly Nucked'.[1] Our boys answered with 'Good King Wenceslas', which they'd learned the first verse of as Waits,[2] collecting coppers from door to door. Unfortunately no one knew more than two verses, because Waits always

---

[1] *Stille Nacht*, German for "Silent Night"
[2] carol-singers

either get a curse or a copper before they reach the third verse.

"Then a Fritz with a megaphone shouts 'Merry Christmas, Wessex!'

"Captain Pomeroy was commanding us. Colonel Baggie had gone sick, second-in-command still on leave, and most of the other officers were young second-lieutenants straight from Sandhurst – we'd taken such a knock, end of October. The Captain was a real gentleman: father, grandfather, and great-grandfather all served in the Wessex. He shouts back: 'Who are you?' And they say that they're Saxons, same as us, from a town called Hully in West Saxony.

"'Will your commanding officer meet me in No-man's-land to arrange a Christmas truce?' the Captain shouts again. 'We'll respect a white flag,' he says.

"That was arranged, so Captain Pomeroy and the Fritz officer, whose name was Lieutenant Coburg, climbed out from their trenches and met half-way. They didn't shake hands, but they saluted, and each gave the other word of honour that his troops wouldn't fire a shot for another twenty-four hours. Lieutenant Coburg explained that his Colonel and all the senior officers were back taking it easy at Regimental HQ. It seems they liked to keep their boots clean, and their hands warm: not like our officers.

"Captain Pomeroy came back pleased as Punch, and said: 'The truce starts at dawn, Wessex; but meanwhile we stay in trenches. And if any man of you dares break the truce tomorrow,' he says, 'I'll shoot him myself, because I've given that German officer my word. All the same, watch out, and don't let go of your bundooks.[1]'"

"That suited us; we'd be glad to get up from them damned fire-steps and stretch our legs. So that night we serenaded the Fritzes with all manner of songs, such as 'I want to go Home!' and 'The Top of the Dixie Lid', and the one about 'Old Von Kluck, He Had a Lot of Men'; and they serenaded us with *Deutschland Über Alles*, and songs to the concertina.

"We scraped the mud off our puttees[2] and shined our brasses, to look a bit more regimental next morning. Captain Pomeroy, meanwhile, goes out again with a flashlight and arranges a Christmas football match – kick-off at 10.30 – to be followed at two o'clock by a burial service for all the corpses what hadn't

[1] muskets
[2] leggings

been taken in because of lying too close to the other side's trenches.

" 'Over the top with the best of luck!' shouts the Captain at 8 a.m., the same as if he was leading an attack. And over we went, a bit shy of course, and stood there waiting for the Fritzes. They advanced to meet us, shouting, and five minutes later, there we were . . .

"Christmas was a peculiar sort of day, if ever I spent one. Hobnobbing with the Hun, so to speak: swapping fags and rum and buttons and badges for brandy, cigars and souvenirs. Lieutenant Coburg and several of the Fritzes talked English, but none of our blokes could sling a word of their bat.

"No-man's-land had seemed ten miles across when we were crawling out on a night patrol; but now we found it no wider than the width of two football pitches. We provided the football, and set up stretchers as goal posts; and the Rev. Jolly, our Padre, acted as ref. They beat us 3–2, but the Padre had showed a bit too much Christian charity – their outside-left shot the deciding goal, but he was miles offside and admitted it soon as the whistle went. And we spectators were spread nearly two deep along the touch-lines with loaded rifles slung on our shoulders.

"We had Christmas dinner in our own trenches, and a German bugler obliged with the mess call – same tune as ours. Captain Pomeroy was invited across, but didn't think it proper to accept. Then one of our sentries, a farmer's son, sees a hare loping down the line between us. He gives a view halloo, and everyone rushes to the parapet and clambers out and runs forward to cut it off. So do the Fritzes. There ain't no such thing as harriers in Germany; they always use shot-guns on hares. But they weren't allowed to shoot this one, not with the truce; so they turned harriers same as us.

"Young Totty Fahy and a Saxon corporal both made a grab for the hare as it doubled back in their direction. Totty catches it by the forelegs and the Corporal catches it by the hindlegs, and they fall on top of it simultaneous.

"Captain Pomeroy looked a bit worried for fear of a shindy about who caught that hare; but you'd have laughed your head off to see young Totty and the Fritz both politely trying to force the carcase on each other! So the Lieutenant and the Captain gets together, and the Captain says: 'Let them toss a coin for it.' But the Lieutenant says: 'I regret that our men will not perhaps understand. With us, we draw straws.' So they picked some withered stems of grass, and Totty drew the long one. He was in our section, and we cooked the hare with spuds that night in a big iron pot borrowed from Duck Farm; but Totty gave the Fritz a couple of bully beef tins, and the skin. Best stoo I ever ate!

"We called 'em 'Fritzes' at that time. Afterwards they were 'Jerries', on account of their tin hats. Them helmets with spikes called *Pickelhaubes* was still the issue in 1914, but only for parade use. In the trenches caps were worn; like ours, but grey, and no stiffening in the top. Our blokes wanted pickelhaubes badly to take their fiancées when they went home on leave; but Lieutenant Coburg says, sorry, all pickelhaubes was in store behind the lines. They had to be content with belt-buckles.

"General French commanded the BEF[1] at the time – decent old stick. Said afterwards that if he'd been consulted about the truce, he'd have agreed for chivalrous reasons. He must have reckoned that whichever side beat, us or the Germans, a Christmas truce would help considerably in signing a decent peace at the finish. But the Kayser's High Command were mostly Prussians, and Lieutenant Coburg told us that the Prussians were against the Truce, which didn't agree with their 'frightfulness' notions; and though other battalions were fraternising with the Fritzes up and down the line that day – but we didn't know it – the Prussians weren't having any. Nor were some English regiments: such as the East Lancs on our right flank and the Sherwood Foresters on the left – when the Fritzes came out with white flags, they fired over their heads and waved 'em back. But they didn't interfere with our party. It was worse in the French line: them Frogs machine-gunned all the 'Merry Christmas' parties . . . Of course, the French go in for New Year celebrations more than Christmas.

"One surprise was the two barrels of beer that the Fritzes rolled over to us from the brewery just behind their lines. I don't fancy French beer; but at least this wasn't watered like what they sold us English troops in the estaminets.[2] We broached them out in the open, and the Fritzes broached another two of their own.

"When it came to the toasts, the Captain said he wanted to keep politics out of it. So he offered them 'Wives and Sweethearts!' which the Lieutenant accepted. Then the Lieutenant

[1] British Expeditionary Force
[2] cafés

proposed 'The King!' which the Captain accepted. There was a King of Saxony too, you see, in them days, besides a King of England; and no names were mentioned. The third toast was 'A Speedy Peace!' and each side could take it to mean victory for themselves.

"After dinner came the burial service – the Fritzes buried their corpses on their side of the line; we buried ours on ours. But we dug the pits so close together that one service did for both. The Saxons had no Padre with them; but they were Protestants, so the Rev. Jolly read the Service, and a German Divinity Student translated for them. Captain Pomeroy sent for the Drummers and put us through that parade in proper regimental fashion: slow march, arms reversed, muffled drums, a union jack and all.

"An hour before dark, a funny-faced Fritz called Putzi came up with a trestle table. He talked English like a Yank. Said he'd been in Ringling's Circus over in the United States. Called us 'youse guys', and put on a hell of a good gaff with conjuring tricks and juggling – had his face made up like a proper clown. Never heard such applause as we gave Herr Putzi!

"Then, of course, our bastard of a Brigadier, full of turkey and plum pudding and mince pies, decides to come and visit the trenches to wish us Merry Christmas! Captain Pomeroy got the warning from Fiddler here, who was away down on light duty at Battalion HQ. Fiddler arrived in the nick, running split-arse across the open, and gasping out: 'Captain, Sir, the Brigadier's here; but none of us hasn't let on about the Truce.'

"Captain Pomeroy recalled us at once. 'Imshi,[1] Wessex!' he shouted. Five minutes later the Brigadier came sloshing up the communication trench, keeping his head well down. The Captain tried to let Lieutenant Coburg know what was happening; but the Lieutenant had gone back to fetch him some warm gloves as a souvenir. The Captain couldn't speak German; what's more, the Fritzes were so busy watching Putzi that they wouldn't listen. So Captain Pomeroy shouts to me: 'Private Green, run along the line and order the platoon commanders from me to fire three rounds rapid over the enemies' heads.' Which I did; and by the time the Brigadier turns up, there wasn't a Fritz in sight.

"The Brigadier, whom we called 'Old Horseflesh', shows a lot of Christmas jollity. 'I was very glad,' he says, 'to hear that

---

[1] "Away with you!" from Arabic, picked up in Egypt

Wessex fusillade, Pomeroy. Rumours have come in of fraternisation elsewhere along the line. Bad show! Disgraceful! Can't interrupt the war for freedom just because of Christmas! Have you anything to report?'

"Captain Pomeroy kept a straight face. He says: 'Our sentries report that the enemy have put up a trestle table in No-man's-land, Sir. A bit of a puzzle, Sir. Seems to have a bowl of goldfish on it.' He kicked the Padre, and the Padre kept his mouth shut.

"Old Horseflesh removes his brass hat, takes his binoculars, and cautiously peeps over the parapet. 'They *are* goldfish, by Gad!' he shouts. 'I wonder what new devilish trick the Hun will invent next. Send out a patrol tonight to investigate.' 'Very good, Sir,' says the Captain.

"Then Old Horseflesh spots something else: it's Lieutenant Coburg strolling across the open between his reserve and front lines; and he's carrying the warm gloves. 'What impudence! Look at that swaggering German officer! Quick, here's your rifle, my lad! Shoot him down point-blank!' It seems Lieutenant Coburg must have thought that the fusillade came from the Foresters on our flank; but now he suddenly stopped short and looked at No-man's-land, and wondered where everyone was gone.

"Old Horseflesh shoves the rifle into my hand. 'Take a steady aim,' he says. 'Squeeze the trigger, don't pull!' I aimed well above the Lieutenant's head and fired three rounds rapid. He staggered and dived head-first into a handy shell-hole.

"'Congratulations,' said Old Horseflesh, belching brandy in my face. 'You can cut another notch in your rifle butt. But what effrontery! Thought himself safe on Christmas Day, I suppose! Ha, ha!' He hadn't brought Captain Pomeroy no gift of whisky or cigars, nor nothing else; stingy bastard, he was. At any rate, the Fritzes caught on, and their machine-guns began traversing tock-tock-tock, about three feet above our trenches. That sent the Brigadier hurrying home in such a hurry that he caught his foot in a loop of telephone wire and went face forward into the mud. It was his first and last visit to the front line.

"Half an hour later we put up an ALL CLEAR board. This time us and the Fritzes became a good deal chummier than before. But Lieutenant Coburg suggests it would be wise to keep quiet about the lark. The General Staff might get wind of it and kick up a row, he says. Captain Pomeroy agrees. Then the Lieutenant warns us that the Prussian Guards are due to relieve his Saxons the day after Boxing Day. 'I suggest that we continue the Truce until then, but with no more fraternisation,' he says. Captain Pomeroy agrees again. He accepts the warm gloves and in return gives the Lieutenant a Shetland wool scarf. Then he asks whether, as a great favour, the Wessex might be permitted to capture the bowl of goldfish, for the Brigadier's sake. Herr Putzi wasn't too pleased, but Captain Pomeroy paid him for it with a gold sovereign and Putzi says: 'Please, for Chrissake, don't forget to change their water!'

"God knows what the Intelligence made of them goldfish when they were sent back to Corps HQ, which was a French luxury *shadow* . . . I expect someone decided the goldfish have some sort of use in trenches, like the canaries we take down the coal pits.

"Then Captain Pomeroy says to the Lieutenant: 'From what I can see, Coburg, there'll be a stalemate on this front for a year or more. You can't crack our line, even with massed machine-guns; and we can't crack yours. Mark my words: our Wessex and your West Saxons will still be rotting here next Christmas – what's left of them.'

"The Lieutenant didn't agree, but he didn't argue. He answered: 'In that case, Pomeroy, I hope we both survive to meet again on that festive occasion; and that our troops show the same gentlemanly spirit as today.'

" 'I'll be very glad to do so,' says the Captain, 'if I'm not scuppered meanwhile.' They shook hands on that, and the truce continued all Boxing Day. But nobody went out into No-man's-land, except at night to strengthen the wire where it had got trampled by the festivities. And of course we couldn't prevent our gunners from shooting; and neither could the Saxons prevent theirs. When the Prussian Guards moved in, the war started again; fifty casualties we had in three days, including young Totty who lost an arm.

"In the meantime a funny thing had happened: the sparrows got wind of the truce and came flying into our trenches for biscuit crumbs. I counted more than fifty in a flock on Boxing Day.

"The only people who objected strongly to the truce, apart from the Brigadier and a few more like him, was the French girls. Wouldn't have nothing more to do with us for a time when we got back to billets. Said we were *no bon* and *boko camarade* with the *Allemans*."[1]

[1] Said we were no good and too friendly with the Germans.

Stan had been listening to this tale with eyes like stars. "Exactly," he said. "There wasn't any feeling of hate between the individuals composing the opposite armies. The hate was all whipped up by the newspapers. Last year, you remember, I attended the Nürnberg Youth Rally. Two other fellows whose fathers had been killed in the last war, like mine, shared the same tent with four German war-orphans. They weren't at all bad fellows."

"Well, lad," I said, taking up the yarn where Dodger left off, "I didn't see much of that first Christmas Truce owing to a spent bullet what went into my shoulder and lodged under the skin: the Medico cut it out and kept me off duty until the wound healed. I couldn't wear a pack for a month, so, as Dodger told you, I got Light Duty down at Battalion HQ, and missed the fun. But the second Christmas Truce, now that was another matter. By then I was Platoon Sergeant to about twenty men signed on for the Duration of the War – some of them good, some of 'em His Majesty's bad bargains.

"We'd learned a lot about trench life that year; such as how to drain trenches and build dug-outs. We had barbed wire entanglements in front of us, five yards thick, and periscopes, and listening posts out at sap-heads;[1] also trench-mortars and rifle-grenades, and bombs, and steel-plates with loop-holes for sniping through.

"Now I'll tell you what happened, and Dodger here will tell you the same. Battalion orders went round to company HQ every night in trenches, and the CO was now Lieut.-Colonel Pomeroy – DSO[2] with bar. He'd won brevet rank for the job he did rallying the battalion when the big German mine blew C-company to bits and the Fritzes followed up with bombs and bayonets. However, when he sent round Orders two days before Christmas 1915, Colonel Pomeroy (accidentally on purpose) didn't tell the Adjutant to include the 'Official Warning to All Troops' from General Sir Douglas Haig. Haig was our new Commander-in-Chief. You hear about him on Poppy Day – the poppies he sowed himself, most of 'em! He'd used his influence with King George, to get General French booted out and himself shoved into the job. His 'Warning' was to the effect that any man attempting to fraternise with His Majesty's enemies on

[1] the foremost end of a trench
[2] Distinguished Service Order

the poor excuse of Christmas would be court-martialled and shot. But Colonel Pomeroy never broke his word, not even if he swung for it; and here he was alongside the La Bassée Canal, and opposite us were none other than the same West Saxons from Hully!

"The Colonel knew who they were because we'd coshed and caught a prisoner in a patrol scrap two nights before, and after the Medico plastered his head, the bloke was brought to Battalion HQ under escort (which was me and another man). The Colonel questioned him through an interpreter about the geography of the German trenches: where they kept that damned minny-werfer,[1] how and when the ration parties came up, and so on. But this Fritz wouldn't give away a thing; said he'd lost his memory when he'd got coshed. So at last the Colonel remarked in English: 'Very well, that's all. By the way, is Lieutenant Coburg still alive?'

" 'Oh, yeah,' says the Fritz, surprised into talking English. 'He's back again after a coupla wounds. He's a Major now, commanding our outfit.'

"Then a sudden thought struck him. 'For Chrissake,' he says, 'ain't you the Wessex officer who played Santa Claus last year and fixed that truce?'

" 'I am,' says the Colonel, 'and you're Putzi Cohen the Conjurer, from whom I once bought a bowl of goldfish! It's a small war!'

"That's why, you see, the Colonel hadn't issued Haig's warning. About eighty or so of us old hands were still left, mostly snobs,[2] bobbajers,[3] drummers, transport men, or wounded blokes rejoined. The news went the rounds, and they all rushed Putzi and shook his hand and asked couldn't he put on another conjuring gaff for them? He says: 'Ask Colonel Santa Claus! He's still feeding my goldfish.'

"I was Putzi's escort, before I happened to have coshed him and brought him in; but I never recognized him without his grease paint – not until he started talking his funny Yank English.

"The Colonel sends for Putzi again, and says: 'I don't think you're quite well enough to travel. I'm keeping you here as a hospital case until after Christmas.'

"Putzi lived like a prize pig the next two days, and put on a

[1] from German *Minenwerfer*, bomb thrower
[2] soldiers employed in cobbling
[3] an Army word for cooks, derived from Hindustani

show every evening – card tricks mostly, because he hadn't his accessories. Then came Christmas Eve, and a sergeant of the Holy Boys[1] who lay on our right flank again, remarked to me it was a pity that 'Stern-Endeavour' Haig had washed out our Christmas fun. 'First I've heard about,' says I, 'and what's more, chum, I don't want to hear about it, see? Not officially, I don't.'

"I'd hardly shut my mouth before them Saxons put out Chinese lanterns again and started singing 'Stilly Nucked'. They hadn't fired a shot, neither, all day.

"Soon word comes down the trench: 'Colonel's orders: no firing as from now, without officer's permission.'

"After stand-to next morning, soon as it was light, Colonel Pomeroy he climbed out of the trench with a white hankerchief in his hand, picked his way through our wire entanglements and stopped half-way across No-man's-land. 'Merry Christmas, Saxons!' he shouted. But Major Coburg had already advanced towards him. They saluted each other and shook hands. The cheers that went up! 'Keep in your trenches, Wessex!' the Colonel shouted over his shoulder. And the Major gave the same orders to his lot.

"After jabbering a bit they agreed that any bloke who'd attended the 1914 party would be allowed out of trenches, but not the rest – they could trust only us regular soldiers. Regulars, you see, know the rules of war and don't worry their heads about politics nor propaganda; them Duration blokes sickened us sometimes with their patriotism and their lofty skiting, and their hatred of 'the Teuton foe' as one of 'em called the Fritzes.

"Twice more Saxons than Wessex came trooping out. We'd strict orders to discuss no military matters – not that any of our blokes had been studying German since the last party. Football was off, because of the overlapping shell holes and the barbed wire, but we got along again with signs and a bit of café French, and swapped fags and booze and buttons. But the Colonel wouldn't have us give away no badges. Can't say we were so chummy as before. Too many of ours and theirs had gone west[2] that year and, besides, the trenches weren't flooded like the first time.

"We put on three boxing bouts: middle, welter and light;

[1] nickname for the Royal Norfolk Regiment
[2] been killed

92

won the welter and light with k.o.s, lost the middle on points. Colonel Pomeroy took Putzi up on parole, and Putzi gave an even prettier show than before, because Major Coburg had sent back for his grease paints and accessories. He used a parrokeet this time instead of goldfish.

"After dinner we found we hadn't much more to tell the Fritzes or swap with them, and the officers decided to pack up before we all got into trouble. The Holy Boys had promised not to shoot, and the left flank was screened by the Canal bank. As them two was busy discussing how long the no-shooting truce should last, all of a sudden the Christmas spirit flared up again. We and the Fritzes found ourselves grabbing hands and form- ing a ring around the pair of them – Wessex and West Saxons all mixed anyhow and dancing from right to left to the tune of 'Here We Go Round the Mulberry Bush', in and out of shell holes. Then our RSM[1] pointed to Major Coburg, and some of our blokes hoisted him on their shoulders and we all sang 'For He's a Jolly Good Fellow'. And the Fritzes hoisted our Colonel up on their shoulders too, and sang *Hock Solla Leeben*, or some- thing . . . Our Provost-sergeant took a photo of that; pity he got his before it was developed.

"Now here's something I heard from Lightning Collins, an old soldier in my platoon. He'd come close enough to overhear the Colonel and the Major's conversation during the middle- weight fight when they thought nobody was listening. The Colonel says: 'I prophesied last year, Major, that we'd still be here this Christmas, what was left of us. And now I tell you again that we'll still be here *next* Christmas, *and* the Christmas after. If we're not scuppered; and that's a ten to one chance. What's more, next Christmas there won't be any more fun and games and fraternisation. I'm doubtful whether I'll get away with this present act of insubordination; but I'm a man of my word, as you are, and we've both kept our engagement.'

" 'Oh, yes, Colonel,' says the Major. 'I too will be lucky if I am not court-martialled. Our orders were as severe as yours.' So they laughed like crows together.

"Putzi was the most envied man in France that day: going back under safe escort to a prison camp in Blighty.[2] And the Colonel told the Major: 'I congratulate you on that soldier.

[1] Regimental Sergeant Major
[2] England

93

He wouldn't give away a thing!'

"At four o'clock sharp we broke it off; but the two officers waited a bit longer to see that everyone got back. But no, young Stan, that's not the end of the story! I had a bloke in my platoon called Gipsy Smith, a dark-faced, dirty soldier, and a killer. He'd been watching the fun from the nearest sap-head, and no sooner had the Major turned his back than Gipsy aimed at his head and tumbled him over.

"The first I knew of it was a yell of rage from everyone all round me. I see Colonel Pomeroy run up to the Major, shouting for stretcher-bearers. Them Fritzes must have thought the job was premeditated, because when our stretcher-bearers popped out of the trench, they let 'em have it and hit one bloke in the leg. His pal popped back again.

"That left the Colonel alone in No-man's-land. He strolled calmly towards the German trenches, his hands in his pockets – being too proud to raise them over his head. A couple of Fritzes fired at him, but both missed. He stopped at their wire and shouted: 'West Saxons, my men had strict orders not to fire. Some coward has disobeyed. Please help me carry the Major's body back to your trenches! Then you can shoot me, if you like; because I pledged my word that there'd be no fighting.'

"The Fritzes understood, and sent stretcher-bearers out. They took the Major's body back through a crooked lane in their wire, and Colonel Pomeroy followed them. A German officer bandaged the Colonel's eyes as soon as he got into the trench, and we waited without firing a shot to see what would happen next. That was about four o'clock, and nothing did happen until second watch. Then we see a flashlight signalling, and presently the Colonel comes back, quite his usual self.

"He tells us that, much to his relief, Gipsy's shot hadn't killed the Major but only furrowed his scalp and knocked him senseless. He'd come to after six hours, and when he saw the Colonel waiting there, he'd ordered his immediate release. They'd shaken hands again, and said: 'Until after the war!', and the Major gives the Colonel his flashlight.

"Now the yarn's nearly over, Stan, but not quite. News of the truce got round, and General Haig ordered first an Inquiry and then a Court Martial on Colonel Pomeroy. He wasn't shot, of course; but he got a severe reprimand and lost five years' seniority. Not that it mattered, because he got shot between the eyes in the 1916 Delville Wood show where I lost my foot.

"As for Gipsy Smith, he said he'd been obeying Haig's strict orders not to fraternise, and also he'd felt bound to avenge a brother killed at Loos. 'Blood for blood,' he said, 'is our gipsy motto.' So we couldn't do nothing but show what we thought by treating him like the dirt he was. And he didn't last long. I sent Gipsy back with the ration party on Boxing Night. We were still keeping up our armed truce with the Saxons, but again their gunners weren't a party to it, and outside the Quartermaster's hut Gipsy got his backside removed by a piece of howitzer shell. Died on the hospital train, he did.

"Oh, I was forgetting to tell you that no sparrows came for biscuit crumbs that Christmas. The birds had all cleared off months before.

"Every year that war got worse and worse. Before it ended, nearly three years later, we'd have ten thousand officers and men pass through that one battalion, which was never at more than the strength of five hundred rifles. I'd had three wounds by 1916; some fellows got up to six before it finished. Only Dodger here came through without a scratch. That's how he got his name, dodging the bullet that had his name and number on it. The Armistice found us at Mons, where we started. There was talk of 'Hanging the Kayser'; but they left him to chop wood in Holland instead. The rest of the Fritzes had their noses properly rubbed in the dirt by the Peace Treaty. But we let them rearm in time for a second war, Hitler's war, which is how your Dad got killed. And after Hitler's war there'd have been a third war, just about now, which would have caught you, Stanley my lad, if it weren't for that blessed bomb you're asking me to march against.

"Now, listen, lad; if two real old-fashioned gentlemen like Colonel Pomeroy and Major Coburg – never heard of him again, but I doubt if he survived, having the guts he had – if two real men like them two couldn't hope for a third Christmas Truce in the days when 'mankind', as you call 'em, was still a little bit civilised, tell me, what can you hope for now?

"Only fear can keep the peace," I said. "The United Nations are a laugh, and you know it. So thank your lucky stars that the Russians have H-bombs and that the Yanks have H-bombs, stacks of 'em, enough to blow your 'mankind' up a thousand times over; and that everyone's equally respectful of everyone else, though not on regular visiting terms."

I stopped, out of breath, and Dodger takes Stan by the hand.

"You know what's right for *you*, lad," he says. "So don't listen to your Grand-dad. Don't be talked out of your beliefs! He's one of the Old and Bold, but maybe he's no wiser nor you and I."

# The Non-Combatant

# The Non-Combatant

**Ian Hay**

*First World War*

We will call the village St Grégoire. That is not its real name;
because the one thing you must not do in war time is to call a
thing by its real name. To take a hackneyed example, you do not
call a spade a spade: you refer to it, officially, as *Shovels, General
Service, One*. This helps to deceive, and ultimately to surprise,
the enemy; and as we all know by this time, surprise is the essence
of successful warfare. On the same principle, if your troops
are forced back from their front-line trenches, you call this
"successfully straightening out an awkward salient".

But this by the way. Let us get back to St Grégoire. Hither,
mud-splashed, ragged, hollow-cheeked, came the Seventh Hairy
Jocks,[1] after four months' continuous employment in the
firing-line. Ypres was a household word to them; Plugstreet was
familiar ground; Givenchy they knew intimately; Loos was
their wash-pot – or rather, a collection of wash-pots, for in
winter all the shell-craters are full to overflowing. In addition
to their prolonged and strenuous labours in the trenches, the
Hairy Jocks had taken a part in a Push – a part not altogether
unattended with glory, but prolific in casualties. They had not
been "pulled out" to rest and refit for over six months, for Divisions on the Western Front were not at that period too numerous,
the voluntary system being at its last gasp, while the legions of
Lord Derby had not yet crystallised out of the ocean of public
talk which held them in solution. So the Seventh Hairy Jocks
were bone tired. But they were as hard as a rigorous winter in
the open could make them, and – they were going back to rest
at last. Had not their beloved CO told them so? And he had
added, in a voice not altogether free from emotion, that if ever
men deserved a solid rest and a good time, "you boys do!"

So the Hairy Jocks trudged along the long, straight, nubbly
French road, well content, speculating with comfortable

---

[1] This and other nicknames in this story are typical of regimental nicknames of
the First World War but have not been identified. They may be inventions.

pessimism as to the character of the billets[1] in which they would find themselves.

Meanwhile, ten miles ahead, the advance party were going round the town in quest of the billets.

Billet-hunting on the Western Front is not quite so desperate an affair as hunting for lodgings at Margate, because in the last extremity you can always compel the inhabitants to take you in – or at least, exert pressure to that end through the *Mairie*. But at the best one's course is strewn with obstacles, and fortunate is the adjutant[2] who has to his hand a subaltern[3] capable of finding lodgings for a thousand men without making a mess of it.

The billeting officer on this, as on most occasions, was one Cockerell – affectionately known to the entire battalion as "Sparrow" – and his qualifications for the post were derived from three well-marked and invaluable characteristics, namely, an imperious disposition, a thick skin, and an attractive *bonhomie* of manner.

Behold him this morning dismounting from his horse in the *place* of St Grégoire. Around him are grouped his satellites – the Quartermaster-Sergeant, four company sergeants, some odd orderlies, and a forlorn little man in a neat drab uniform with light blue facings – the regimental interpreter. The party have descended, with the delicate care of those who essay to perform acrobatic feats in kilts, from bicycles – serviceable but appallingly heavy machines of Government manufacture, the property of the "Buzzers",[4] but commandeered for the occasion. The Quartermaster-Sergeant, who is not accustomed to strenuous exercise, mops his brow and glances expectantly round the square. His eye comes gently to rest upon a small but hospitable-looking *estaminet*.[5]

Lieutenant Cockerell examines his wrist-watch.

"Half-past ten!" he announces. "Quartermaster-Sergeant!"

"Sirr!" The Quartermaster-Sergeant unglues his longing gaze from the *estaminet* and comes woodenly to attention.

"I am going to see the Town Major about a billeting area. I will meet you and the party here – in twenty minutes."

[1] quarters
[2] an officer who assists superior officers in the details of military duty
[3] an officer of junior rank
[4] Army slang for a portable telephone, here probably referring to a signalling unit
[5] café

Master Cockerell trots off on his mud-splashed steed, followed by the respectful and appreciative salutes of his followers – appreciative, because a less considerate officer would have taken the whole party direct to the Town Major's office and kept them standing in the street, wasting moments which might have been better employed elsewhere, until it was time to proceed with the morning's work.

"How strong are you?" inquired the Town Major.

Cockerell told him. The Town Major whistled.

"That all? Been doing some job of work, haven't you?"

Cockerell nodded, and the Town Major proceeded to examine a large-scale plan of St Grégoire, divided up into different coloured plots.

"We are rather full up at present," he said, "but the Cemetery Area is vacant. The Seventeenth Geordies moved out yesterday. You can have that." He indicated a triangular section with his pencil.

Master Cockerell gave a deprecatory cough.

"We have come here, sir," he intimated dryly, "for a change of scene."

The stout Town Major – all town majors are stout – chuckled.

"Not bad for a Scot!" he conceded. "But it's quite a cheery district, really. You won't have to doss down in the cemetery itself, you know. These two streets here" – he flicked a pencil – "will hold practically all your battalion, at its present strength. There's a capital house in the Rue Jean Jacques Rousseau which will do for Battalion Head-quarters. The corporal over there will give you your *billets de logement*."[1]

"Are there any other troops in the area, sir?" asked Cockerell, who, as already indicated, was no child in these matters.

"There ought not to be, of course. But you know what the Heavy Gunners and the ASC.[2] are. If you come across any of them, fire them out. If they wear too many stars and crowns[3] for you, let me know, and I will perform the feat myself. You fellows need a good rest and no worries, I know. Good morning."

At ten minutes to eleven Cockerell found the Quartermaster-Sergeant and party, wiping their moustaches and visibly refreshed, at the exact spot where he had left them; and the hunt for billets began.

---

[1] tickets assigning quarters to the soldiers
[2] Army Service Corps
[3] indications of officers' ranks

"A" Company were easily provided for, a derelict tobacco factory being encountered at the head of the first street. Lieutenant Cockerell accordingly detached a sergeant and a corporal from his train, and passed on. The wants of "B" Company were supplied by commandeering a block of four dilapidated houses farther down the street – all in comparatively good repair except the end house, whose roof had been disarranged by a shell during the open fighting in the early days of the war.

This exhausted the possibilities of the first street, and the party debouched[1] into the second, which was long and straggling, and composed entirely of small houses.

"Now for a bit of the retail business!" said Master Cockerell resignedly. "Sergeant M'Nab, what is the strength of 'C' Company?"

"One hunner and thairty-fower other ranks, sirr," announced Sergeant M'Nab, consulting a much-thumbed roll book.

"We shall have to put them in twos and threes all down the street," said Cockerell. "Come on: the longer we look at it the less we shall like it. Interpreter!"

The forlorn little man, already described, trotted up, and saluted with open hand, French fashion. His name was Baptiste Bombominet ("or words to that effect", as the adjutant put it), and may have been so inscribed upon the regimental roll; but throughout the rank and file Baptiste was affectionately known by the generic title of "Alphonso". The previous seven years had been spent by him in the congenial and blameless atmosphere of a Ladies' Tailors in Hanover Square, where he enjoyed the status and emoluments of chief cutter. Now, called back to his native land by the voice of patriotic obligation, he found himself selected, by virtue of a residence of seven years in England, to act as official interpreter between a Scottish regiment which could not speak English and Flemish peasants who could not speak French. No wonder that his pathetic brown eyes always appeared full of tears. However, he followed Cockerell down the street, and meekly embarked upon a contest with the lady inhabitants thereof in which he was hopelessly outmatched from the start.

At the first door a dame of massive proportions, but keen business instincts, announced her total inability to accommodate *soldats*, but explained that she would be pleased to entertain

[1] emerged

*officiers* to any number. This is a common gambit. Twenty British privates in your *grenier*,[1] though extraordinarily well behaved as a class, make a good deal of noise, buy little, and leave mud everywhere. On the other hand, two or three officers give no trouble, and can relied upon to consume and pay for uncounted omelettes and bowls of coffee.

That seasoned vessel, Lieutenant Cockerell, turned promptly to the sergeant and corporal of "C" Company.

"Sergeant M'Nab," he said, "you and Corporal Downie will billet here." He introduced hostess and guests by an expressive wave of the hand. But shrewd Madame was not to be bluffed.

"*Pas de sergeants, Monsieur le Capitaine!*" she exclaimed. "*Officiers!*"

"*Ils sont officiers – sous-officiers,*" explained Cockerell, rather ingeniously, and moved off down the street.

At the next house the owner – a small, wizened lady of negligible physique but great staying power – entered upon a duet with Alphonso which soon reduced that very moderate performer to breathlessness. He shrugged his shoulders feebly, and cast an appealing glance towards the lieutenant.

"What does she say?" inquired Cockerell.

"She says dis 'ouse no good sair! She 'ave seven children, and one *malade* – seek."

"Let me see," commanded the practical officer.

He insinuated himself as politely as possible past his reluctant opponent, and walked down the narrow passage into the kitchen. Here he turned, and inquired:

"Er – *où est la pauvre petite chose?*"

Madame promptly opened the door, and displayed a little girl in bed – a very flushed and feverish little girl.

Cockerell grinned sympathetically at the patient, to that young lady's obvious gratification; and turned to the mother.

"*Je suis très – triste,*" he said, "*j' ai grand misericorde. Je ne placerai pas de soldats ici. Bon jour!*"

By this time he was in the street again. He saluted politely and departed, followed by the grateful regards of Madame.

No special difficulties were encountered at the next few houses. The ladies at the house door were all polite; many of them were most friendly; but naturally each was anxious to

[1] attic

get as few men and as many officers as possible – except the proprietress of an *estaminet*, who offered to accommodate the entire regiment. However, with a little tact here and a little firmness there, Master Cockerell succeeded in distributing "C" Company among some dozen houses.

One old gentleman, with a black alpaca cap and a sixday's beard, proprietor of a lofty establishment at the corner of the street, proved not only recalcitrant, but abusive. With him Cockerell dealt promptly.

"*Ca suffit!*" he announced. "*Montrez-moi votre grenier!*"[1]

The old man, grumbling, led the way up numerous rickety staircases to the inevitable loft under the tiles. This proved to be a noble apartment thirty feet long. From wall to wall stretched innumerable strings.

"We can get a whole platoon in here," said Cockerell contentedly. "Tell him, Alphonso. These people," he explained to Sergeant M'Nab, "always dislike giving up their lofts, because they hang their laundry there in winter. However, the old boy must lump it. After all, we are in this country for his health, not ours; and he gets paid for every man who sleeps here. That fixes 'C' Company. Now for 'D'! The other side of the street this time."

Quarters were found in due course for "D" Company; after which Cockerell discovered a vacant building site which would serve for transport lines. An empty garage was marked down for the Quartermaster's ration store, and the Quartermaster-Sergeant promptly faded into its recesses with a grateful sigh. An empty shop in the Rue Jean-Jacques Rousseau, conveniently adjacent to Battalion Head Quarters, was appropriated for that gregarious band, the regimental signallers and telephone section; while a suitable home for the anarchists, or bombers, together with their stock-in-trade, was found in the basement of a remote dwelling on the outskirts of the area.

After this, Lieutenant Cockerell, left alone with Alphonso and the orderly in charge of his horse, heaved a sigh of exhaustion and transferred his attention from his notebook to his watch.

"That finishes the rank and file," he said. "I breakfasted at four this morning, and the battalion won't arrive for a couple of hours yet. Alphonso, I am going to have an omelette some-

---

[1] "That's enough!" he announced. "Show me your attic!"

where. I shall want you in half an hour exactly. Don't go wandering off for the rest of the day, pinching soft billets for yourself and the Sergeant-Major and your other pals, as you usually do!"

Alphonso saluted guiltily – evidently the astute Cockerell had "touched the spot" – and was turning away, when suddenly the billeting officer's eye encountered an illegible scrawl at the very foot of his list.

"Stop a moment, Alphonso! I have forgotten those condemned machine-gunners, as usual. *Strafe* them! Come on! Once more unto the breach, Alphonso! There is a little side alley down here that we haven't tried."

The indefatigable Cockerell turned down the *Impasse Gambetta*, followed by Alphonso, faint but resigned.

"Here is the very place!" announced Cockerell almost at once. "This house, Number Five. We can put the gunners and their little guns into that stable at the back, and the officer can have a room in the house itself. *Sonnez*, for the last time before lunch!"

The door was opened by a pleasant-faced young woman of about thirty, who greeted Cockerell – tartan is always popular with French ladies – with a beaming smile, but shook her head regretfully upon seeing the *billet de logement* in his hand. The inevitable duet with Alphonso followed. Presently Alphonso turned to his superior.

"Madame is ver' sorry, sair, but an *officier* is here already."

"Show me the officer!" replied the prosaic Cockerell.

The duet was resumed.

"Madame say," announced Alphonso presently, "that the *officier* is not here now, but he will return."

"So will Christmas! Meanwhile I am going to put an Emma Gee[1] officer in here."

Alphonso's desperate attempt to translate the foregoing idiom into French was interrupted by Madame's retirement into the house, whither she beckoned Cockerell to follow her. In the front room she produced a frayed sheet of paper, which she proffered with an apologetic smile. The paper said:

"*This billet is entirely reserved for the Supply Officer of this District. It is not to be occupied by troops passing through the town. – By Order.*"

Lieutenant Cockerell whistled softly and vindictively through

---

[1] machine-gunner

his teeth.

"Well," he said, "for consummate and concentrated nerve, give me the underlings of the ASC! This potbellied blighter not only butts into an area which doesn't belong to him, but actually leaves a chit to warn people off the grass even when he isn't here! He hasn't signed the document, I observe. That means that he is a newly-joined subaltern trying to get mistaken for a Brass Hat! I'll fix *him!*"

With great stateliness Lieutenant Cockerell tore the offending screed into four portions, to the audible concern of Madame. But the Lieutenant smiled reassuringly upon her.

"*Je vous donnerai un autre, vous savez*," he assured her.

He sat down at the table, tore a leaf from his Field Service Pocket Book, and wrote:

"*The Supply Officer of the District is at liberty to occupy this billet only at such times as it is not required by the troops of the Combatant Services.*

"*Signed, F. J. Cockerell,*
"*Lieut. & Asst. Adj.,*
"*7th B. & W. Highers.*"

"That's a pretty nasty one!" he observed with relish. Then, having pinned the insulting document conspicuously to the mantelpiece, he observed to the mystified lady of the house:

"*Voilà, Madame. Si l' officier reviendra, je le verrai moi-même, avec grand plaisir. Bon jour!*"

And with this dark saying Sparrow Cockerell took his departure.

II

The Battalion, headed by their tatterdemalion[1] pipers, stumped into the town in due course, and were met on the outskirts by the billeting party, who led the various companies to their appointed place. After inspecting their new quarters, and announcing with gloomy satisfaction that they were the worst, dirtiest, and most uncomfortable yet encountered, everybody settled down in the best place he could find, and proceeded to make himself remarkably snug.

Battalion Headquarters and the officers of "A" Company were billeted in an imposing mansion which actually boasted a

[1] ragged and bedraggled

bathroom. It is true that there was no water, but this deficiency was soon made good by a string of officers' servants bearing buckets. Beginning with the CO, who was preceded by an orderly bearing a small towel and a large loofah, each officer performed a ceremonial ablution;[1] and it was a collection of what the second-in-command termed "bright and bonny young faces" which assembled round the Mess table at seven o'clock.

It was in every sense a gala meal. Firstly, it was weeks since anyone (except Second-Lieutenant M'Corquodale, newly joined and addressed, for painfully obvious reasons, as "Tich") had found himself at table in an apartment where it was possible to stand upright. Secondly, the Mess president had coaxed glass tumblers out of the ancient *concierge*; and only those who have drunk from enamelled ironware for weeks on end can appreciate the pure joy of escape from the indeterminate metallic flavour which such vessels impart to all beverages. Thirdly, these same tumblers were filled to the brim with inferior but exhilarating champagne – purchased, as they euphemistically put it in the Supply Column, "locally". Lastly, the battalion had several months of hard fighting behind it, probably a full month's rest before it, and the conscience of duty done and recognition earned floating like a halo above it. For the moment memories of Nightmare Wood and the Kidney Bean Redoubt[2] – more especially the latter – were effaced. Even the sorrowful gaps in the ring round the table seemed less noticeable.

The menu, too, was almost pretentious. First came the *hors d'œuvres* – a tin of sardines. This was followed by what the Mess corporal described as a savoury omelette, but which the second-in-command condemned on the first whiff.

"It is false economy," he observed dryly to the Mess president, "to employ Mark One[3] eggs as anything but hand grenades."

However, the tide of popular favour turned with the haggis, contributed by Lieutenant Angus M'Lachlan, from a parcel from home. Even the fact that the Mess cook, an inexperienced aesthete from Islington, had endeavoured to tone down the naked repulsiveness of the dainty with discreet festoons of tinned macaroni, failed to arouse the resentment of a purely

[1] wash
[2] A redoubt is a last retreat in the field, fortified on all sides.
[3] In the British army each issue of arms or equipment receives a distinctive "Mark". Mark One denotes the earliest issue.

Scottish Mess. The next course – the beef ration, hacked into the inevitable gobbets and thinly disguised by a sprinkling of curry powder – aroused no enthusiasm; but the unexpected production of a large tin of Devonshire cream, contributed by Captain Bobby Little, relieved the canned peaches of their customary monotony. Last of all came a savoury – usually described as *the* savoury – consisting of a raft of toast per person, each raft carrying an abundant cargo of fried potted meat and provided with a passenger in the shape of a recumbent sausage.

A compound of grounds and dishwater, described by the optimistic Mess corporal as coffee, next made its appearance, mitigated by a bottle of Cointreau and a box of Panatellas; and the Mess turned itself to more intellectual refreshment. A heavy and long-overdue mail had been found waiting at St Grégoire. Letters had been devoured long ago. Now, each member of the Mess leaned back in his chair, straightened his weary legs under the table, and settled down, cigar in mouth, to the perusal of the *Spectator* or the *Tatler*, according to rank and literary taste.

Colonel Kemp, unfolding a week-old *Times*, looked over his glasses at his torpid disciples.

"Where is young Sandeman?" he inquired.

Young Sandeman was the adjutant.

"He went out to the orderly room, sir, five minutes ago," replied Bobby Little.

"I only want to give him tomorrow's orders. No doubt he'll be back presently. I may as well mention to you fellows that I propose to allow the men three clear days' rest, except for bathing and reclothing. After that we must do company drill, good and hard, so as to polish up the new draft, who are due tomorrow. I am going to start a bombing school, too; at least seventy-five per cent of the battalion ought to pass the test before we go back to the line. However, we need not rush things. We should be here in peace for at least a month. We must get up some sports, and I think it would be a sound scheme to have a sing-song one Saturday night. I was just saying, Sandeman" – this to the adjutant, who re-entered the room at that moment – "that it would be a sound—"

The adjutant laid a pink field-telegraph slip before his superior.

"This has just come in from Brigade Headquarters, sir," he said. "I have sent for the Sergeant-Major."

The colonel adjusted his glasses and read the despatch. A

deathly, sickening silence reigned in the room. Then he looked up.

"I am afraid I was a bit previous," he said quietly. "The Royal Stickybacks have lost the Kidney Bean, and we are detailed to go up and retake it. Great compliment to the regiment, but a trifle mistimed! You young fellows had better go to bed. Parade at 4 a.m., sharp! Goodnight! Come along to the orderly room, Sandeman."

The door closed, and the Mess, grinding the ends of their cigars into their coffee-cups, heaved themselves resignedly to their aching feet.

"There ain't," quoted the senior major, "no word in the blooming language for it!"

III

The Kidney Bean Redoubt is the key to a very considerable sector of trenches.

It lies just behind a low ridge. The two horns of the bean are drawn back out of sight of the enemy, but the middle swells forward over the skyline and commands an extensive view of the country beyond. Direct observation of artillery fire is possible; consequently an armoured observation post has been constructed here, from which gunner officers can direct the fire of their batteries with accuracy and elegance. Lose the Kidney Bean, and the boot is on the other leg. The enemy has the upper ground now: he can bring observed artillery fire to bear upon all our tenderest spots behind the line. He can also enfilade[1] our front-line trenches.

Well, as already stated, the Twenty-Second Royal Stickybacks had lost the Kidney Bean. They were a battalion of recent formation, stouthearted fellows all, but new to the refinements of intensive trench warfare. When they took over the sector, they proceeded to leave undone various vital things which the Hairy Jocks had always made a point of doing, and to do various unnecessary things which the Hairy Jocks had never done. The observant Hun promptly recognised that he was faced by a fresh batch of opponents, and, having carefully studied the characteristics of the newcomers, prescribed and administered an exemplary dose of frightfulness. He began by tickling up the Stickybacks with an unpleasant engine called

[1] to rake with fire from end to end

the *Minenwerfer*, which despatches a large sausage-shaped projectile in a series of ridiculous somersaults high over no-man's-
land into the enemy's front-line trench, where it explodes and
annihilates everything in that particular bay. Upon these
occasions one's only chance of salvation is to make a rapid
calculation as to the bay into which the sausage is going to fall,
and then double speedily round a traverse[1] – or, if possible, two
traverses – into another. It is an exhilarating pastime, but
presents complications when played by a large number of
persons in a restricted space, especially when the persons
aforesaid are not unanimous as to the ultimate landing place of
the projectile.

After a day and a night of these aerial torpedoes the Hun
proceeded to an intensive artillery bombardment. He had long
coveted the Kidney Bean, and instinct told him that he would
never have a better opportunity of capturing it than now.
Accordingly, two hours before dawn, the Redoubt was subjected
to a sudden, simultaneous, and converging fire from all the
German artillery for many miles round, the whole being topped
up with a rain of those crowning instruments of demoralisation,
gas shells. At the same time an elaborate curtain of shrapnel
and high explosive was let down behind the Redoubt, to serve
the double purpose of preventing either the sending up of
reinforcements or the temporary withdrawal of the garrison.

At the first streak of dawn the bombardment was switched
off, as if by a tap; the curtain fire was redoubled in volume,
and a massed attack swept across the disintegrated wire into
the shattered and pulverised Redoubt. Other attacks were
launched on either flank; but these were obvious blinds, in-
tended to prevent a too concentrated defence of the Kidney
Bean. The Royal Stickybacks – what was left of them – put up
a tough fight; but half of them were lying dead or buried, or
both, before the assault was launched, and the rest were too
dazed and stupefied by noise and chlorine gas to withstand –
much less to repel – the overwhelming phalanx[2] that was
hurled against them. One by one they went down, until the
enemy troops, having swamped the Redoubt, gathered themselves up in a fresh wave and surged towards the reserve-line
trenches, four hundred yards distant. At this point, however,

[1]  right-angle bend in a trench
[2]  solid formation of soldiers

they met a strong counter attack, launched from the Brigade Reserve, and after heavy fighting were bundled back into the Redoubt itself. Here the German machine-guns had staked out a defensive line, and the German retirement came to a standstill.

Meanwhile a German digging party, many hundred strong, had been working madly in no-man's-land, striving to link up the newly acquired ground with the German lines. By the afternoon the Kidney Bean was not only "reversed and consolidated", but was actually included in the enemy's front-trench system. Altogether a well planned and admirably executed little operation.

Forty-eight hours later the Kidney Bean Redoubt was re-captured.

Many arms of the Service took honourable part in the enterprise – heavy-guns, field-guns, trench-mortars, machine-guns; sappers and pioneers, infantry in various capacities. But this narrative is concerned only with the part played by the Seventh Hairy Jocks.

"Sorry to pull you back from rest, Colonel," said the Brigadier, when the Commander of the Hairy Jocks reported; "but the Divisional General considers that the only feasible way to hunt the Boche from the Kidney Bean is to bomb him out of it. That means trench fighting, pure and simple. I have called you up because you fellows know the ins and outs of the place as no one else does. Here is an aeroplane photograph of the Redoubt, as at present constituted. Tell off your own bombing parties; make your own dispositions; send me a copy of your provisional orders; and I will fit my plan in with yours. The Corps Commander has promised to back you with every gun, trench-mortar, culverin[1] and arquebus[2] in his possession."

In due course battalion orders were issued and approved. They dealt with operations most barbarous amid localities of the most home-like sound. Number Nine Platoon, for instance (Commander, Lieutenant Cockerell), were to proceed in single file, carrying so many grenades per man, up Charing Cross Road, until stopped by the barrier which the enemy were understood to have erected in Trafalgar Square, where a bombing-post and at least one machine-gun would probably be encountered. At this point they were to wait until Trafalgar

[1]  cannon
[2]  portable fire-arm

Square had been suitably dealt with by a trench-mortar. (Here followed a paragraph addressed exclusively to the Trench-Mortar officer.) After this the bombers of Number Three Platoon would bomb their way across the Square and up the Strand. Another party would clear Northumberland Avenue, while a Lewis-gun raked Whitehall. And so on. Every detail was thought out, down to the composition of the parties which were to "clean up" afterwards – that is, extract the reluctant Boche from various underground fastnesses well known to the extractors. The whole enterprise was then thoroughly rehearsed in some dummy trenches behind the line, until every one knew his exact part. Such is modern warfare.

Next day the Kidney Bean Redoubt was in British hands again. The Hun – what was left of him after an intensive bombardment of twenty-four hours – had betaken himself back over the ridge, *via* the remnants of his two new communication trenches, to his original front line. The two communication trenches themselves were blocked and sandbagged, and were being heavily supervised by a pair of British machine-guns. Fighting in the Redoubt itself had almost ceased, though a humorous sergeant, followed by acolytes[1] bearing bombs, was still combing out certain residential districts in the centre of the maze. Ever and anon he would stoop down at the entrance of some deep dug-out, and bawl:

"Ony mair doon there? Come away, Fritz! I'll gie ye five seconds. Yin, Twa, Three—"

Then, with a rush like a bolt of rabbits, two or three close-cropped, grimy creatures would scuttle up from below and project themselves from one of the exits; to be taken in charge by grinning Caledonians wearing tin hats very much awry, and escorted back through the barrage to the "prisoners' base" in rear.

All through the day, amidst unremitting shell-fire and local counter attack, the Hairy Jocks reconsolidated the Kidney Bean; and they were so far successful that when they handed over the work to another battalion at dusk, the parapet was restored, the machine-guns were in position, and a number of "knife-rest" barbed-wire entanglements were lying just behind the trench, ready to be hoisted over the parapet and joined together in a continuous defensive line as soon as the night was sufficiently dark.

---

[1] junior attendants

One by one the members of Number Nine Platoon squelched – for it had rained hard all day – back to the reserve line. They were utterly exhausted, and still inclined to feel a little aggrieved at having been pulled out from rest; but they were well content. They had done the State some service, and they knew it; and they knew that the higher powers knew it too. There would be some very flattering reading in Divisional orders in a few days' time.

Meanwhile, their most pressing need was for something to eat. To be sure every man had gone into action that morning carrying his day's rations. But the British soldier, improvident as the grasshopper, carries his day's rations in one place, and one place only – his stomach. The Hairy Jocks had eaten what they required at their extremely early breakfast: the residue thereof they had abandoned.

About midnight Master Cockerell, in obedience to a most welcome order, led the remnants of his command, faint but triumphant, back from the reserve line to a road junction two miles in rear, known as the Dead Dog Corner. Here the battalion were to *rendezvous*, and march back by easy stages to St Grégoire. Their task was done.

But at the crossroads Number Nine Platoon found no battalion: only a solitary subaltern with his orderly. This young Casabianca informed Cockerell that he, Second-Lieutenant Candlish, had been left behind to "bring in stragglers".

"Stragglers?" exclaimed the infuriated Cockerell. "Do we look like stragglers, damn you?"

"No," replied the youthful Candlish frankly; "you look more like sweeps. However, you had better push on. The battalion isn't far ahead. The order is to march straight back to St Grégoire and reoccupy former billets."

"What about rations?"

"Rations? The Quartermaster was waiting here for us when we *rendezvoused*, and every man had a full ration and a tot of rum." (Number Nine Platoon cleared their parched throats expectantly.) "But I fancy he has gone on with the column. However, if you leg it you should catch them up. They can't be more than two miles ahead. So long!"

IV

But the task was hopeless. Number Nine Platoon had been bombing, hacking, and digging all day. Several of them were slightly wounded – the serious cases had been taken off long ago by the stretcher bearers – and Cockerell's own head was still dizzy from the fumes of a German gas shell.

He lined up his disreputable paladins[1] in the darkness, and spoke:

"Sergeant M'Nab, how many men are present?"

"Eighteen, sirr." The platoon had gone into action thirty-four strong.

"How many men are deficient of an emergency ration? I can make a good guess, but you had better find out."

Five minutes later the sergeant reported. Cockerell's guess was correct. The British private has only one point of view about the portable property of the State. To him, as an individual, the sacred emergency ration is an unnecessary encumbrance, and the carrying thereof a "fatigue". Consequently when engaged in battle, one of the first (of many) things which he jettisons is that very ration. When all is over, he reports with unctuous solemnity that the provender in question has been blown out of his haversack by a shell. The Quartermaster-Sergeant writes it off as "lost owing to the exigencies of military service", and indents for another.

Lieutenant Cockerell's haversack contained a packet of meat lozenges and about half a pound of chocolate. These were presented to the Sergeant.

"Hand these round as far as they will go, Sergeant," said Cockerell. "They'll make a mouthful a man, anyhow. Tell the platoon to lie down for ten minutes; then we'll push off. It's only fifteen miles. We ought to make it by breakfast time . . . "

Slowly, mechanically, all through the winter night the victors hobbled along. Cockerell led the way, carrying the rifle of a man with a wounded arm. Occasionally he checked his bearings with a map and electric torch. Sergeant M'Nab, who, under a hirsute[2] and attenuated exterior, concealed a constitution of ferro-concrete and the heart of a lion, brought up the rear, uttering fallacious assurances to the faint-hearted as to the shortness of the distance now to be covered, and carrying two rifles.

The customary halts were observed. At ten minutes to four the men flung themselves down for the third time, at a cross-roads. They had covered about seven miles, and were still eight

[1] knightly heroes
[2] hairy

or nine from St Grégoire. The everlasting constellation of Verey lights still rose and fell upon the eastern horizon behind them, but the guns were silent.

"There might be a heavy battery dug in somewhere about here," mused Cockerell. "I wonder if we could touch them for a few tins of bully. Hallo, what's that?"

A distant rumble came from the north, and out of the darkness loomed a British motor lorry, lurching and swaying along the rough cobbles of the *pavé*. Some of Cockerell's men were lying dead asleep in the middle of the road, right at the junction. The lorry was going twenty miles an hour.

"Get into the side of the road, you men!" shouted Cockerell, "or they'll run over you. You know what these MT[1] drivers are!"

With indignant haste, and at the last possible moment, the kilted figures scattered to either side of the narrow causeway. The usual stereotyped and vitriolic remonstrances were hurled after the great hooded vehicle as it lurched past.

And then a most unusual thing happened. The lorry slowed down, and finally stopped, a hundred yards away. An officer descended, and began to walk back. Cockerell rose to his weary feet and walked to meet him.

The officer wore a major's crown upon the shoulder straps of his sheepskin-lined British Warm and the badge of the Army Service Corps upon his cap. Cockerell, indignant at the manner in which his platoon had been hustled off the road, saluted stiffly, and muttered: "Good morning, sir!"

"Good morning!" said the major. He was a stout man of nearly fifty, with twinkling blue eyes and a short, clipped moustache. Cockerell judged him to be one of the few remnants of the original British Army.

"I stopped," explained the older man, "to apologise for the scandalous way that fellow drove over you. It was perfectly damnable; but you know what these converted taxi-drivers are! This swine forgot for the moment that he had an officer on board, and hogged it as usual. He goes under arrest as soon as we get back to billets."

"Thank you very much, sir," said Master Cockerell, entirely thawed. "I'm afraid my chaps were lying all over the road; but they are pretty well down and out at present."

[1] Military Transport

"Where have you come from?" inquired the major, turning a curious eye upon Cockerell's prostrate followers.

Cockerell explained. When he had finished, he added wistfully:

"I suppose you have not got an odd tin or two of bully to give away, sir? My fellows are about—"

For answer, the Major took the Lieutenant by the arm and led him towards the lorry.

"You have come," he announced, "to the very man you want. I am practically Sir Thomas Lipton.[1] In fact, I am a Corps Supply officer. How would a maconochie[2] apiece suit your boys?"

Cockerell, repressing the ecstatic phrases which crowded to his tongue, replied that that was just what the doctor had ordered.

"Where are you bound for?" continued the Major.

"St Grégoire."

"Of course. You were pulled out from there, weren't you? I am going to St Grégoire myself as soon as I have finished my round. Home to bed, in fact. I haven't had any sleep worth writing home about for four nights. It's no joke tearing about a country full of shell holes, hunting for people who have shifted their ration dump seven times in four days. However, I suppose things will settle down again, now that you fellows have fired Brother Boche out of the Kidney Bean. Pretty fine work, too! Tell me, what is your strength, here and now?"

"One officer", said Cockerell soberly, "and eighteen other ranks."

"All that's left of your platoon?"

Cockerell nodded. The stout Major began to beat upon the tailboard of the lorry with his stick.

"Sergeant Smurthwaite!" he shouted.

There came a muffled grunt from the recesses of the lorry. Then a round and ruddy face rose like a harvest moon above the tailboard, and a stertorous voice replied respectfully:

"Sir?"

"Let down this tailboard; take this officer's platoon into the lorry; issue them with a maconochie and a tot of rum apiece; and don't forget to put Smee under arrest for dangerous driving

---

[1] founder of the chain of Liptons grocery stores
[2] a tinned ration of sliced vegetables, mainly turnips and carrots, with a lot of gravy or soup

when we get back to billets."

"Very good, sir."

Ten minutes later the survivors of Number Nine Platoon, soaked to the skin, dazed, slightly incredulous, but at peace with all the world, reclined close-packed and steaming upon the floor of the swaying lorry. Each man held an open tin of Mr Maconochie's admirable ration between his knees. Perfect silence reigned; a pleasant aroma of rum mellowed the already vitiated atmosphere.

In front, beside the chastened Mr Smee, sat the major and Master Cockerell. The latter had just partaken of his share of refreshment, and was now endeavouring, with lifeless fingers to light a cigarette.

The Major scrutinized his guest intently. Then he stripped off his British Warm coat – incidentally revealing the fact that he wore upon his tunic the ribbons of both South African medals and the Distinguished Service Order – and threw it round Cockerell's shoulders.

"I'm sorry, boy!" he said. "I never noticed. You are chilled to the bone. Button this round you."

Cockerell made a feeble protest, but was cut short.

"Nonsense! There's no sense in taking risks after you've done your job."

Cockerell assented, a little sleepily. His allowance of rum was bringing its usual vulgar but comforting influence to bear upon an exhausted system.

"I see you have been wounded, sir," he observed, noting with a little surprise two gold stripes upon his host's left sleeve – the sleeve of a "non-combatant".

"Yes," said the Major. "I got the first one at Le Cateau. He was only a little fellow; but the second, which arrived at the Second Show at Ypres, gave me such a stiff leg that I am only an old crock now. I was second-in-command of an infantry battalion in those days. In these, I am only a peripatetic[1] grocer. However, I am lucky to be here at all; I've had twenty-seven years' service. How old are you?"

"Twenty," replied Cockerell. He was too tired to feel as ashamed as he usually did at having to confess to the tenderness of his years.

The Major nodded thoughtfully.

[1] itinerant, wandering

"Yes," he said. "I judged that would be about the figure. My son would have been twenty this month, only – he was at Neuve Chapelle. He was very like you in appearance – very. His mother would have been interested to meet you. You might as well take a nap for half an hour. I have two more calls to make, and we shan't get home till nearly seven. Lean on me, old man: I'll see you don't tumble overboard . . . "

So Lieutenant Cockerell, conqueror of the Kidney Bean, fell asleep, his head resting, with scandalous disregard for military etiquette, upon the shoulder of the stout Major.

v

An hour or two later, Number Nine Platoon, distended with concentrated nourishment and painfully straightening its cramped limbs, decanted itself from the lorry into a little cul-de-sac opening off the Rue Jean Jacques Rousseau in St Grégoire. The name of the cul-de-sac was the *Impasse Gambetta*.

Their commander, awake and greatly refreshed, looked round him and realised, with a sudden sense of uneasiness, that he was in familiar surroundings. The lorry had stopped at the door of Number Five.

"I don't suppose your battalion will get back for some time," said the major. "Tell your sergeant to put your men into the stable behind this house – there's plenty of straw there – and –"

"Their own billet is just round the corner, sir," replied Cockerell. "They might as well go there, thank you."

"Very good. But come in with me yourself, and doss here for a few hours. You can report to your CO later in the day, when he arrives. This is my *pied-à-terre*" – rapping on the door. "You won't find many billets like it. As you see, it stands in this little backwater, and is not included in any of the regular billeting areas of the town. The Town Major has allotted it to me permanently. Pretty decent of him, wasn't it? And Madame Vinot is a dear. Here she is! *Bonjour Madame Vinot! Avez-vous un feu –* er – *inflammé pour moi dans la chambre?*" Evidently the major's French was on a par with Cockerell's.

But Madame understood him, bless her!

"*Mais oui, M' sieur le Colonel!*" she exclaimed cheerfully – the rank of major is not recognized by the French civilian population – and threw open the door of the sitting-room, with a glance of compassion upon the major's mud-splashed companion, whom she failed to recognise.

A bright fire was burning in the open stove.

Immediately above, pinned to the mantelpiece and fluttering in the draught, hung Cockerell's manifesto upon the subject of non-combatants. He could not recognise his own handwriting across the room. The Major saw it too.

"Hallo, what's that hanging up, I wonder?" he exclaimed. "A memorandum for me, I expect; probably from my old friend Dados.[1] Let us get a little more light."

He crossed to the window and drew up the blind. Cockerell moved too. When the Major turned round, his guest was standing by the stove, his face scarlet through its grime.

"I'm awfully sorry, sir," said Cockerell, "but that notice – memorandum – of yours has dropped into the fire."

"If it came from Dados," replied the Major, "thank you very much!"

"I can't tell you, sir," added Cockerell humbly, "what a fool I feel."

But the apology referred to an entirely different matter.

---

[1] DADOS: Deputy Assistant Director of Ordnance Supplies

Going Home

# Going Home

**James S. Kenary**

*Vietnam War*

He came in feeling good. It's funny, he thought, that I should be feeling this way, but what the hell, I'll be going home now, and my wound isn't so bad that it will be with me forever. The medics rushed Will from the chopper, stopping momentarily to check his leg, then moved inside and set him on a rack in a small, makeshift emergency room. He moved his head stiffly to one side and was suddenly frightened by the sight of a massive, fat man peppered with red marks ringed in blue and with thick, white patches on his eyes. It was hard for him to look at the man, so he turned away, but he could still hear the hard, sputtering gasps of his breathing, and he felt very sorry and sick.

The nurses came by and cut away his clothing and his boots that dripped blood in a trail along the floor, and then a young, pale doctor put a needle into the bend in his arm and attached a bottle of clear fluid to a metal pole above his stretcher. Without his clothes he felt cold, but he did not mention it because he was finally safe, and he did not want to lose that. A nurse stopped by him and punched a needle into his upper arm and he smiled into her face. She smiled too, and rushed away as quickly as she had come. He apologised for not having worn underwear, but she had gone and did not hear him.

The room was crowded with wounded men after the attack, and Will liked the excitement and the security. He wished that one of the nurses would spend some time with him, touch him, but none of them could stop. His blood was rushing through him madly and he felt fully alive like after an attack when all of them would come together and talk about it wildly.

A medic, starched and uneasy, approached him clutching a clip-board.

"Can you talk?" he asked timidly.

"Sure," Will said, glad to have a release. "What do you need?"

"I've got to get some information as long as you're able to talk."

120

"Okay."

"What's your name?"

"Garrett, William S."

"Service number?"

"Two-two-three-eight-seven-nine-eight."

"Would you like anyone to be notified of this?"

"No," Will said sharply. "Underline that, will you?"

"Don't worry. No one will be notified."

"That's the main thing, okay? Make sure of it, will you?"

"Sure. Really. Don't worry about it." The medic looked at Will for the first time, expression grave, as if trying to understand the intensity of the demand.

A nurse went by, then stopped and looked back at Will. He felt good having her eyes on him, but it did not excite him in a sexual way. It was the same feeling he had had when the small village girls had clung to him as he passed through their streets, then watched him move away.

"I'm sorry about not having worn underwear, Nurse," he called, raising himself with his elbows. "I don't wear any in the bush. None of us do. Anyway, I didn't plan on this."

"That's all right. I've seen it before. Just don't make it a habit."

Will laughed with the nurse and was suddenly ecstatic with the affection in her voice, the security of the room, and the knowledge that soon he would be going home. He would settle for the clean comfort of the hospital for a few days, but not for longer, because still there would be the distance, the immeasurable space between the war and the dream, and until that had been closed, nothing could soothe his fear.

Another man was carried in and set down next to Will. He recognised him as someone from his own unit who had gotten it from the same round, and whom he had tried to help before realising that his own leg was hit and immovable. He had not known him, well, but now he felt that they were very close and wanted desperately to console him.

"Hey, Bart? How are you feeling?"

Bart groaned, almost wailed. Will was frightened by the transformation that had taken place in him since the wound. The sobbing and the writhing and the setting had changed him into another man, an apparition, and his face seemed relined and misshapen. He was incomplete, formless, as if something more than skin and blood and bone had been torn from his body, and Will thought sadly that he would never know him as he had been before this day.

"Are you okay, Bart?" Will leaned toward him. "Do you want me to call someone?"

"Did it go through?" Bart asked, teeth clenched and caked with dried dirt and pieces of brush. "Can you see if it went through?"

"You mean through your leg? I'll look." Will hung over the edge of his stretcher. He could not see well through the thick, clotted blood, but he knew that it had gone through and that only a few pieces of the leg were left. He looked away and worked himself squarely back onto his stretcher. A hard clod burned in his throat. He turned his head toward Bart again who was lying with his eyes shut, his parched lips moving, searching for saliva.

"It's okay, Bart. It didn't go through. You're going to be all right. Really."

The nurses were around Bart now and they seemed worried as they prepared him for surgery. He cried, sensing the urgency, but a medic jabbed a needle into his arm, and after a short, spasmodic fit of trembling, his body relaxed and his head dropped limply to the side. Will felt better that Bart was unconscious, but he could hear that the fat man was dying and he wanted to be taken away from the death.

He had seen a man die once before – an enemy – and had remembered it clearly since then, especially in the night when he had tried to sleep it away. They had found him on a trail, pushed like heaped clothing to the side, and his breathing had been like the fat man's, enormous explosions of sputtering life, and his legs and his chest had moved convulsively. They had all stopped and watched him die, and some had even laughed toughly through it, jabbing and kicking at the dying man. Will was remembering that now as he listened to the sporadic bursts of half-life next to him, and he did not want to see it again, or to be near it. He called a medic.

"He's dying, medic," he whispered.

The medic nodded. "Yeah, I know."

"Can't you move him?"

"No room now. We'll have to wait," he said moving away. "It won't be long."

The medic was gone and Will knew that he would have to see it and hear it and remember it again. His leg began to throb and burn, and the coolness of the room became damp. He could hear the fat man going, and the nurses were suddenly next to him with a doctor, and there were muffled voices combined with gasps, and then it was very quiet, except for the rustling of a sheet and the wooden sounds of the stretcher.

Will was uncomfortable next to the dead man. It seemed that a wet coldness came from that side, a gnawing, persistent reminder of the death, of its finality, and Will shivered, his naked body defenceless against the severe chill. For a long time, he waited on his stretcher listening to the *hack-hacking* of the choppers outside and to the moaning and the crying and the frightened laughter in the room. He looked at the ceiling, not wanting to see any more of the wounded men, or the nurses who were too busy for him. He tried to forget the pain in his leg and wished that he could sleep or dream of going home. But his mind and his body were tense, inflexible, and would not allow it. He still relished the cleanness and security of the hospital, but he had lost the ecstasy he had felt in the beginning when its detachment and its safety had been new, and when the nurse had stopped to joke and laugh with him.

Finally two medics rolled him onto a movable stretcher and pushed him down a hallway full of thick heat into a small, steaming room.

"X-ray," the medic announced. "Give this to the doctor when he gets to you." He handed Will a manila envelope.

Will started to ask a question, but the medic had gone. He had wanted to know why he was being treated this way, why the nurses hadn't grouped around him, talked to him, touched him, why he was being made to hold his own records. I'm wounded, he thought. I shouldn't have to do this. How about a little consideration, or do I have to be dying to get that? Maybe if I had my leg shot off like Bart. That might do it. That might at least earn me a pat on the head. Oh, cut this out. Forget it. I'm going home. That's all that matters. I've got a good wound. If the nurses don't have time for me, the hell with it. I'll be out of here in a few days anyway.

The doctor came and asked to see Will's records. Will was glad to have some attention.

"So you got it in the leg, huh? How's it feel?" the doctor asked.

"Not too bad. It burns a little."

"Well, we'll take a look at it and see how deep the piece is, okay?" The doctor turned. "Medic, wheel this man into X-ray."

The medic pushed Will into the dark room. "You're going to have to get up on the table so I can get a picture. Can you move by yourself or are you going to need some help?" His voice was cold.

"I can do it." You arrogant bastard, Will thought. I wouldn't let you help me if both my legs were shot off. Will pulled himself slowly, painfully, onto the table, dragging his bad leg across the stretcher. The burning intensified with movement and he closed his teeth and his eyes, battling the pain and the indignation. They're making me pay for it, he thought, watching the stiff leg slide sluggishly along the table. Going home is never easy when the wound is a good one.

After the X-rays had been taken and given to Will in the manila envelope, he was wheeled to the pre-op room, a noiseless tomb that seemed to have a pain of its own. A nurse greeted him, took the envelope, and looked firmly into his eyes. He could feel a loosening process take place, a gentle, flowing heat that moved along the senses, relaxing them, obscuring the injustice, and he smiled thankfully in return.

"Aren't you cold?" she asked. "You must be freezing with this air-conditioning the way it is. I'll get you a blanket." She left briskly, and Will sat up slightly to watch her. She wasn't pretty, but she had a special beauty that came from the moment and from his need for her. She looked strange in the green clothes and jungle boots, but they didn't matter. None of that mattered now as it had once before.

She returned with a blanket and covered Will. "The doctor will be here soon," she said. "We've all been pretty busy."

"I know," Will said. "This was the worst it's ever been. They must have hit us with everything they had."

"I hope it ends soon." She sighed, lowering her eyes.

"Why are you here?"

"I guess it's because of my brother. He was killed here." She looked at Will; her face showed a composed sadness. "At first I came here because of him, but now it's for something else. It wasn't right when it was only for him." She smiled easily, as if from some exclusive knowledge or recollection.

Will was watching her so closely that he was not aware of the silence. He was studying the smile and the eyes and the thin, fine lines that trailed delicately beneath them. The mouth still held the smile, as one holds onto hope, and the eyes were bright and clear.

"I hope it ends soon too," he said finally, disrupting the silence. "I don't want any more of it."

"It will." She touched his head lightly.

He was sorry when she left, but his body was loose and relaxed now, and he had forgotten the bad treatment. He closed his eyes and waited for the doctor. More men were being carried in on stretchers and he listened to the movement. Some were crying and swearing strongly, others were quiet, pensive, like himself.

The doctor came and looked briefly at Will's wound without speaking. Here we go with the cold treatment again, Will thought, but his bitterness had ebbed because of the nurse, and he looked into the light on the ceiling that hung swaying with the air of the room. He wanted it to end. Take the piece, sew the wound, and send me home. That's all. Do it fast and well, and then I'll leave you. I'll just forget some of the bad treatment because I know what a strain it must be taking care of all these guys. I realise how hard it must be to watch them crying and dying and going home. I understand. So I'll forget it. Just fix me up, and I'll be gone, because I've got a going home wound.

"Are you sleeping?" Will heard the nurse's voice, as if from a vast, peaceful distance. He opened his eyes.

"I'm going to wash your wound now so that the doctor can look for the fragment." She smiled and Will was warmed again. He lifted his head to watch her work, but not to see the wound.

"How does it look?" he asked.

"Good. It's a clean wound, but it may be deep."

"I'll be glad to have it out," he said looking beyond her to a stretcher being wheeled from the operating room. He could not see the face of the man on it, but he knew that it was Bart. He watched the medics for a sign, an indication of Bart's condition, but their expressions were tired and vacant, and revealed nothing. The condition of all men is the same to them, Will thought. Blood and skin, life or death. That is why I cannot read their faces. But I know that it is bad. I can feel that myself without having to watch them, and I am sorry that I never knew him until the wound, because now it is too late.

"Do you know anything about him?" Will motioned toward the stretcher with his eyes.

"Who?" The nurse looked up.

"That one. The one they're wheeling out."

"He lost his leg." She faced Will. "Do you know him?"

"He was in my unit. I tried to help him today, but I couldn't move."

"There was nothing left of it. They would have saved it if they could, but it was almost all gone." Her eyes closed for an instant before she looked down.

"I know. I saw it. I told him it was all right. But he knew that I was lying. Maybe I should have told him the truth."

"No." Her head came up sharply. "You were right. He'll know the truth soon enough, and if he remembers, he'll forgive you."

Will felt her working on his leg, and despite the pain, he wanted her to go on. The rubbing of the cloth against the wound drove heat into his thigh, and stabbing, steel-like pains into his knee and ankle and foot, but the hand that did not work, except to hold his leg steady and to comfort him, seemed to stop the worst of it, the agony, from moving further than the wound itself. It could have forced its way into his system and made him suffer, but she controlled it with her hand and her touch, and the pain was good because it let him feel her more. His eyes without his mind watched the light above him. If only he could carry this with him – this good, comfortable feeling from the nurse – and use it to get him by the details, it could be very easy. Stay with me, he begged silently. Make it easy for me, and I'll take you away from the war. But that's not what you want, is it? You told me about it before and I could sense then that you loved it here, that, for you, this is more important than going home. You have come here to calm and soothe, and to watch the grateful faces of men like myself, and if that is what you want and need, then I am all for it, if only somehow I could keep it exclusively until I am home. But that would be selfish, and I could not ask you to stay by me alone. And so, I will have to leave without you, but I will always remember your love for this place as compared to my contempt, and because you have shown it to me so clearly, I will understand.

She finished with the cleaning and went to find the doctor. The leg was cool where the wet cloths had been pressed, but without her hands rubbing and moving there, the pain began to run beyond the wound, surging hotly, then icily, then hotly and icily again and again in flashing repetitions that made the heat and the cold the same, indistinguishable. He shut his eyes and felt anger tears forming and a damp hardness in his throat that would make them come unless he could stop the thrust now before it took him over. Think of it, he thought. It's almost here. What you've been waiting for. Going home. The doctor will come to tell you soon. He'll say it when he sees the wound. "Well, it looks like you're going home with this one," he'll say. And you won't smile too wide, because you don't want to lose it now. So you'll just nod and sigh and close your eyes and say, "Yeah, I guess so," but inside you'll be repeating the words, celebrating them, and you'll know that it has finally come – the beginning of the going home process – and you will suddenly be sure of keeping your life, and be beautifully on your way. On your way home.

Will continued to imagine how the process would be, and how he would pass through each separate stage of the trip home. When he could think of it no longer, because of the anxiety that was beginning to sicken him in the stomach, he sat up and scanned the room. He liked it now only because it seemed invulnerable, separate from the war and the world, surrounded by cold space. But he hated it for its lifelessness and its well-scoured dullness, and he wondered if men who might have lived died because of it. He was angry that those who worked here had never noticed the passive quality of the walls, had never thought to paint them, to make them more alive, more hopeful. The room had the same stillness as the places he had been just before or after battle, and it did not help a man to recover, or to want to recover. It's because none of them here know how it is in the bush, he thought, that they make it like this. If they knew, they would change it, and more men would live or recover because of it. But maybe they don't want it that way. And as much as he hated to think of that, he felt that it might be true, that possibly there was a reason for the deathly colour of this room, and suddenly he believed it and was frightened.

The nurse was next to him and his fear. "Are you afraid?" She bent close to him.

"I don't know." He fell back on his stretcher. "I've just been thinking and it hasn't done me much good."

"Do you want something? Something to make you sleep?"

"No." He breathed more easily. "Not that. What I really need is to be on my way home. That's all that can help me, except your being here, which is a damn good substitute."

"I guess that's what all of us need."

He did not like the answer because of its righteousness, and he looked away, eyes closed.

"The doctor should have been here," she said, as if aware that she had been too curt. "But he's terribly busy, and there's been some bad wounds."

"I'll wait."

"Are you sure you're all right?"

"I'm fine," he said, then turned to watch her go.

He was asleep when the doctor came and did not feel the needle that was pumping in his leg to numb it. He wanted to be more awake, but he could not return easily, and he felt that he was losing some of the goodness and the excitement of the process. His eyes fluttered between sleep and consciousness; he could not hold or control them. He perceived only in stages and felt nothing. There was a great distance from him to the doctor, who was at the wound, and an even greater distance from there to the end of his leg that he could see vaguely, as if it were a part of the wall, or another body. He wanted it closer to himself. He wanted the total experience, from the beginning to the end, because now it was for him, finally and surely for him. For too long it had been withheld and he had begun to think that he might never have it, but now with the wound and the removal from the war, he knew that a change was taking place.

The doctor was working with difficulty, and Will was jarred by the pulling and the digging in his leg. There was no feeling, only rough movement. He lay still and wooden, more confident, more in control than he could remember since the day that he had been taken and prepared for war. He was certain that he was on his way now, and he was anxiously happy. He wondered how long the doctor would work and how big the piece would be. He wondered too about the words he would be told with, how they would sound, how he would react. It was coming closer. All of it was a service to him now, a preparation. I'll let it happen, he thought. I'll just lie here, and then when the words come I'll play it out right, and from there, they can wheel me through the rest of it. It will be slow, and I'll worry through it, but it will be nothing like the bush and the searching and the hurting. Now, if only it would start, I would feel better, and I could prepare myself for all of it, because even though it is what I want and need and love, it will not be easy.

And when the doctor stopped working and seemed finished, Will tensed with the excitement of the impending announcement. The doctor looked tired. His eyes were set deep and framed roughly with wild, scowling lines like trenches. Will hated and respected him immediately.

"How do you feel?" he asked Will with a voice that seemed to come from somewhere other than his mouth.

"Not too bad."

"I'm sorry we didn't get to you sooner, but we've had so many worse ones that we had to take them according to their condition."

"That's okay. Did you get the piece?"

"No, I couldn't find it." The doctor frowned. "It must be deep, and it's probably not worth going in after. Sometimes it does more harm than good, digging through all that muscle."

"You mean I'm always going to have it in my leg?"

"Maybe not. A lot of times shrapnel will work its way right through the skin. One day it might just pop out," he said smiling. "Your piece may stay there, though, because it's very deep. Scar tissue will form around it, and it will probably be there for the rest of your life." The doctor seemed pleased to be giving the details.

"What about infection?" Will asked. "Could it get infected?"

"It could, but it's not likely. When the shrapnel entered your leg it was so hot it was sterile. Actually you're very lucky. It looks good, and you shouldn't be bothered by it after it heals."

The doctor went to the end of the stretcher and picked up the chart that had been left there. He wrote in it hurriedly, occasionally lifting his eyes to study the wound while Will lay silently watching his abrupt, professional movements, hating them terrifically, but depending on them to keep his hope alive. When the doctor had finished writing he called a nurse and handed her the folder. He glanced once again at Will's wound, then walked away quickly. Suddenly, as if remembering a small obligation, he spun and returned to Will.

"Okay!" He slapped Will heavily on the good leg. "You can go back to your unit now. Stop by in about four days and we'll sew you up. We have to leave the wound open for awhile in case of infection."

Will tensed and smiled incredulously at the doctor who was ready to leave, to discard his case without sending him home. If he had not planned so carefully the details of his trip home, if he had not created the stages so precisely, he could have turned and strained for a moment, allowing the truth to settle. But he had projected beyond his limit, had built a certainty from a hope and a need.

"You want me to go back to my unit?" Will asked.

"Can you get someone to pick you up?" The doctor did not feel the plea.

"I don't know. I guess so," Will stammered. "They were pretty well scattered when I left, but there should be someone around. Can I call from here?"

"Sure. Right over there."

"Do you think the piece will ever have to come out?"

"I don't think so. It shouldn't bother you much. There might be some nerve damage, but it will only be minor."

How can I say it, Will thought. How can I tell him what I want? Please doctor, send me home. I'll pay for it. I'll send money to you for the rest of my life. Just let me out of here, I've seen enough, I'll never make it. They'll get me again. There was a time when I thought I couldn't be hit. But I've lost that now, and I'm terrified. I'm fucking terrified. What stops me from telling you, begging you? I shouldn't care what you think. I can't go out there again, that's all. There's nothing left to prove. I'm a target now, a wounded, limping fear-target, and every-thing is pointed at me. They'll get me for sure. I can't escape them. Come on! Say it! Tell him how you feel. Tell him you can't go back out there. Tell him you won't.

The doctor broke the pause. "Is there anything else I can do?"

Will was roused from the warring in his mind. "No. No, thank you. I'll be all right, I guess. I'll be back in four days."

"Good. I'll see you then." The doctor rushed away, leaving Will shaken and weak, a great, scalding wetness in his eyes. He tried to rise and sit, but the trembling in his body stopped him, and he fell back, working to control the outrage. His eyes were closed to restrain the rush of tears that he could feel coming, his arms were up across his face to hide the breakdown. He waited for the torrent to burst and overwhelm him, but mysteriously it lost its intensity, and he could feel its stinging dissipation, its dryness, and suddenly he was alone with the realisation that he was not going home.

He lay motionless, arms still across his eyes, until he could think of it no longer. The room was almost empty now, and he sat up slowly, squint-eyed, forcing movement, hating it, wincing from the pain. He stretched his legs out fully in front of him, testing them for strength. Why couldn't I tell him? Why couldn't I explain to him how I feel? He might have let me go. It might have been easy. If I had asked him, I would have known. But

I was afraid. Of what he'd think? Of my own cowardice? Haven't I learned anything here? None of that matters anymore. Staying alive is all that is important. But I used to do the same thing in the bush. We'd come back in to the rear area and get together at night, and I'd say I'm never going back out there again. And then, the next day when the order came down and all of them started putting their gear together and grumbling about the war, I'd do it too, and I'd go right back out there and get into it again. Won't I ever learn? It's like a curse, and the worst thing about it is that someday it might just kill me.

Will lifted his good leg over the edge of the stretcher and let it hang down loosely. He watched it swing, freely, easily, and thought of the other leg, stiff and hot, and of how difficult it would be to move. When he was ready, he stretched the good leg to the floor and put his weight on it, at the same time sliding the other one cautiously to the edge of the stretcher. The burning started with the pulling, and when he had finally dragged it over and down, the pain was more severe than if he had set it into a deep fire. He dropped his head.

The nurse saw his pain and came to him.

"Can I help?" She bent to see his face.

"I think I'm going to need some crutches and something to wear."

"You mean the doctor didn't give you anything?"

Will shook his head in his hand, then looked up, eyes fierce. "No, he didn't give me anything. Not a goddamn thing."

"Well, I'll get you some, okay? I'll be right back."

Will dropped his head again, sorry that he had shown his contempt. The nurse returned immediately with the crutches, and he took them indifferently.

"The medic is getting you some pants," she said. "We're all out of shirts."

"It doesn't matter."

"I hope you'll be all right."

Will did not respond. He knew that he could not have her any more. The medic brought the pants.

"Can I help?" the nurse asked.

"You can hold the crutches."

He bent at the waist and strained, fitting the bad leg into the pants. The other leg went in more easily, but the burning was greater from the shift of weight. When he stood up, his face was fever red, and he turned away from the nurse as he buttoned his pants, calming himself.

"Will you be back to see the doctor?" she asked.

"In four days." Will struggled forward.

"Maybe I'll see you then." She moved next to him.

"Maybe."

At the door she left him, and he did not watch her or look back into the barren room. He leaned heavily on his crutches, squeezing the handgrips until the heels of his palms were chafed, but he did not reach for the door. Instead, he thought of what he had lost, of what the war would be like now that he had come so close to being removed from it. Without this, he thought, I could have made it, but now that I have seen it and touched it and it has fooled me, I am not right for going back. Oh Christ, I hate to think of leaving here. I cannot control my fear. It has me completely, and I'm only moving because I have not yet died. But I will die. I'm sure of it. They'll destroy my chance to live again, to return home. Oh God, what can I do?

Will opened the door brashly and was struck with a rush of light and heat that held all of it again – the discomfort, the lethargy, the uselessness – and it sucked in at him, as air would push into a vacuum. For a moment, he floundered in the brilliance of the sunlit hallway, attempting to adjust to the sudden change.

When he could see clearly, he stopped and looked down the narrow hallway. Standing against the wall opposite him were two of them – the lieutenant and the Top.[1] They had come to take him back. Will froze, afraid to face them, afraid to submit himself once more to their authority. He saw their pallid faces, despising them, possessed entirely now by the horror of the return. They hated him. He knew that. They had come only as a formality. Their offer of concern, their willingness to help, was nothing more than a means of priming him for recovery, of keeping as many men as possible between them and the war.

They didn't even wait for my call, Will thought. They're frantic. And so, now I've lost my chance to return to the unit at my own pace. I could have made my way back slowly, but now that they are here to pick me up, it is too late. I cannot fool myself any longer. They will take me – the ones who make it worse than the actual war, the ones that made the war for all of us – and now it will never be the same. Oh God, I hate to

---

[1] the sergeant

think of going back, of fighting it again, of losing it. The leg will heal and they will watch it and know when I am ready, and although I'll try to hide it, I will not evade their plan. They'll send me out again and I'll remember all of it as it was – the going home process. The whole of it. And I will think only of how close it seemed to take me to the proper distance from the war land, how close I seemed to home.

Will did not speak to them. He did not have to, now. He had something more than they had, something because of them, and he accused them with his silence. They went outside to bring the truck around, and Will moved slowly down the long hallway toward the intense brightness at the end. He could see it in the open door and remember the feel of it and how it had burned his eyes. He knew that he would be in it soon, just as he had been in it before the wound, and now, convinced at last that the possibility of escape was finally gone, and that he would never have it again, the crying began, first with a series of spasms, then with weaknesses in his legs, and then with an explosion of tears that dropped him to the floor in a heap like the man he had seen on the trail that day and had not been able to cry for.

# The Raid

# The Raid

**Alun Lewis**

*Second World War*

My platoon and I were on training that morning. We've been on training every morning for the last three years, for that matter. On this occasion it was Current Affairs, which always boils down to how long the war is going to last, and when the orderly told me the CO wanted me in his office I broke the lads off for a cup of tea from the charwallah[1] and nipped over to the orderly room, tidying myself as I went. I didn't expect anything unusual until I took a cautionary peep through the straw window of his matting shed and saw a strange officer in there. So I did a real dapper salute and braced myself. Self-defence is always the first instinct, self-suspicion the second. But I hadn't been drunk since I came to India and I hadn't written anything except love in my letters. As for politics, as far as they're concerned I don't exist, I'm never in. The other chap was a major and had a red armband.

"Come in, Selden," the colonel said. "This is the DAPM.[2] Head of military police. Got a job for you. Got your map case?"

"No, sir. It's in company office."

"Hurry off and fetch it."

When I came back they were hard at it, bending over the inch map. The CO looked up. His face got very red when he bent.

"Here's your objective, Selden. This village here, Chandanullah. Eighteen miles away. Route: track south of Morje, river-bed up to Pimpardi, turn south a mile before Pimpardi and strike across the watershed on a fixed bearing. Work it out with a protractor on the map and set your compass before you march off. Strike the secondary road below this group of huts here, 247568, cross the road and work up the canal to the village. Throw a cordon round the village with two sections of your platoon. Take the third yourself and search the houses methodically. Government has a paid agent in the village who

[1] someone who makes or sells tea
[2] District Assistant Provost Marshal

136

will meet you at this canal bridge here – got it? – at o6.oo hours. The agent reported that your man arrived there last night after dark and is lying up in one of the hovels."

"What man, sir?" I asked.

"Christ, didn't I tell you? Why the devil didn't you stop me? This fellow, what's-his-name – it's all on that paper there – he's wanted. Remember the bomb in the cinema last Tuesday, killed three British other ranks? He's wanted for that. Read the description before you go. Any questions so far? Right. Well, you'll avoid all houses, make a detour round villages, keep off the road all the way. Understand? News travels faster than infantry in India. He'll be away before you're within ten miles if you show yourself. Let's see. Twenty miles by night. Give you ten hours. Leave here at 19.30 hours. Arrive an hour before first light. Go in at dawn, keep your eyes skinned. MT will RV[1] outside the village at dawn. Drive the prisoner straight to jail. DAPM will be there."

"Very good, sir. Dress, sir?" I said.

"Dress? PT shoes, cloth caps, overalls, basic pouches, rifles, fifty rounds of .303 per man and grenades. Sixty-nine grenades if he won't come out, thirty-six grenades if he makes a fight of it. Anything else?"

"No, sir."

"Good. Remember to avoid the villages. Stalk him good and proper. Keep up-wind of him. I'm picking you and your platoon because I think you're the best I've got. I want results, Selden."

"I'll give you a good show, sir."

"Bloody good shot with a .22, Selden is," the CO said to the DAPM by way of light conversation. "Shot six mallard with me last Sunday."

"Of course we want the man alive, sir, if it's at all possible," the DAPM said, fiddling with his nervous pink moustache. "He's not proved guilty yet, you see, sir, and with public opinion in India what it is."

"Quite," said the colonel. "Quite. Make a note of that, Selden. Tell your men to shoot low."

"Very good, sir."

"Got the route marked on your talc?"[2]

"Yes, sir." I'd marked the route in chinograph[3] pencil and

[1] motor transport will rendezvous
[2] a transparent map-case
[3] a type of crayon

the Chandanullah place in red as we do for enemy objectives. It was all thick.

"Rub it all off, then. Security. Read his description. Have you read it? What is it?"

"Dark eyes, sir. Scar on left knee. Prominent cheekbones. Left corner of mouth droops. Front incisor discoloured. Last seen wearing European suit, may be dressed in native dhoti, Mahratta style."

"And his ring?" said the C.O. He's as keen as mustard, the old man is.

"Oh yes, sir. Plain gold wedding ring."

"Correct. Don't forget these details. Invaluable sometimes. Off with you."

I saluted and marched out.

"Damn good fellow, Selden," I heard the CO say. "Your man is in the bag."

I felt pretty pleased with that. Comes of shooting those six mallard.

The platoon was reassembling after their tea and I felt pretty important, going back with all that dope. After all, it was the first bit of action we'd seen in two and a half years. It would be good for morale. I knew they'd moan like hell, having to do a twenty-mile route march by night, but I could sell them that all right. So I fell them in in threes and called them to attention for disciplinary reasons and told them they'd been picked for a special job and this was it . . .

They were very impressed by the time I'd finished.

"Any questions?" I said.

"Yes, sir," said Chalky White. He was an LPTB[1] conductor and you won't find him forgetting a halfpenny. "Do we take haversack rations and will we be in time for breakfast?" He thinks the same way as Napoleon.[2]

"Yes," I said. "Anything else?"

"What's this fellow done, sir?" Bottomley asked then. Bottomley always was a bit Bolshie, and he's had his knife into me for two and half years because I was a bank clerk in Civvy Street and played golf on Sundays.

"Killed three troops, I think," I said. "Is that good enough?"

I felt I'd scored pretty heavy over his Red stuff this time.

---

[1] London Passenger Transport Board
[2] Napoleon is reported to have said that an army marches on its stomach

"Right," I said. "Break off till 19.00 hours. Keep your mouths shut. White will draw rations at the cookhouse. No cigarettes or matches will be taken."

I did that for disciplinary purposes. They didn't say a word. Pretty good.

We crossed the start line dead on 19.30 hours and everybody looked at us with some interest. I felt mighty "hush-hush." My security was first class. Hadn't told a soul, except Ken More and Ted Paynter.

"Bring 'em back alive," a soldier jeered outside the cookhouse.

Somebody's let the cat out of the bag. Damn them all. Can't trust a soul in the ranks with the skin of a sausage.

Anyway, we got going bang away. I knew the first stretch past Morje and Pimpardi, and we did about three miles an hour there. The night was breathless and stuffy; we put hankies round our foreheads to keep the sweat out of our eyes. And the perpetual buzzing of the crickets got on my nerves like a motor horn when the points jam and all the pedestrians laugh. I suppose I was a bit worked up. Every time a mosquito or midge touched me I let out a blow fit to knacker a bull. But I settled down after a while and began to enjoy the sense of freedom and deep still peace that informs the night out in the tropics. You've read all about tropical stars; well, it's quite true. They're marvellous; and we use some of them for direction-finding at night too. The Plough, for instance, and one called Cassiopeia that you bisect for the Pole Star.

Then there was the tricky bit over the mountain by compass. I just hoped for the best on that leg. Luckily the moon came up and put the lads in a good mood. I allowed them to talk in whispers for one hour and they had to keep silent for the next hour for disciplinary reasons. We halted for half an hour on the crest of the watershed and ate our bully beef sandwiches with relish, though bully tastes like a hot poultice out here. It was a damn fine view from that crest. A broad valley a thousand feet below with clusters of fires in the villages and round a hill temple on the other side. Either a festival or a funeral, obviously. I could hear the drums beating there, too; it was very clear and echoing, made my flesh creep. You feel so out of it in India somehow. You just slink around in the wilds and you feel very white and different. I don't know . . . You know, I'd have said that valley *hated* us that night, on those rocky crests. Queer.

I didn't know which group of huts was which, but I could see the canal glittering in the moonlight so I was near enough right, praise be. The jackals were howling too, and some creature came right up to us, it gave me a scare. I knew that bully had a pretty bad stench. Anyway we got on the move again, Chalky White saying, "Next stop Hammersmiff Bridge," and we slithered down as quietly as we could, hanging on to each other's rifles on the steep bits. We made our way between the villages and the drums beat themselves into a frenzy that had something personal about it. Then we went up the canal for about four miles, keeping about a hundred yards off the path and pretty rough going it was. Then we came to what I felt must be our objective, a cluster of crumbled huts on the foothills, pretty poor show even for these parts, and the boys were blistered and beat so I scattered them under the bushes and told them to lie low. It was only 5.30 a.m., and the agent fellow wasn't due until six. I had a nap myself, matter of fact, though it's a shootable offence. I woke up with a start and it was five past six, and I peered round my tree and there wasn't a sound. No drums, no jackals, no pie dogs.[1] It was singing in my ears, the silence, and I wished to God we'd got this job over. It could go wrong so easily. He might fight, or his pals might help him, or he might have got wind of us, or I might have come to the wrong place. I was like an old woman. I loaded my Colt and felt better. Then I went down the canal to look for the chowkey fellow.[2] I took a pretty poor view of a traitor, but I took a poorer view of him not turning up. He wasn't there and I walked up the path, and just when I was getting really scared he appeared out of nowhere and I damn near shot him on the spot.

"Officer sahib huzzoor," he said. "Mai Sarkar ko dost hai," or something. And he said the name of the man I was after, which was the password.

"Achiba," I said, meaning *good show*. "Tairo a minute while I bolo my phaltan and then we'll jao jillo." He got the idea.

I nipped back and roused the lads quietly from under the trees and we moved up like ghosts on that village. I never want to see that village again. It was so still and fragile in the reluctant grey light. Even the pie dogs were asleep, and the bullocks lying on their sides. Once I travelled overnight from Dieppe to Paris

[1] stray mongrels
[2] police informer

and the countryside looked just as ghostly that morning. But this time it was dangerous. I had a feeling somebody was going to die and there'd be a hell of a shemozzle. And at the same time the houses looked so poor and harmless, almost timid somehow. And the chowkey bloke was like a ghost. It was seeing him so scared that put me steady again. He was afraid of being seen with us as far as I could make out, and said he'd show us where this fellow was lying up and then he'd disappear, please. I said never mind about the peace, let's get the war over first, and I told Bottomley to watch the bloke in case he had anything up his sleeve.

We got to the ring of trees outside the village without a sound, and the two section leaders led their men round each side of the village in a pincer movement. All the boys were white and dirty and their eyes were like stones. I remember suddenly feeling very proud of them just then.

I gave them ten minutes to get into position and close the road at the rear of the village. And then a damned pie dog set up a yelp over on the right flank and another replied with a long shivering howl. I knew things would start going wrong if I didn't act quickly. We didn't want the village to find out until we'd gone if possible. For political reasons. And for reasons of health, I thought. So I gave the Follow-me sign and closed in on the huddled houses. There were a couple of outlying houses with a little shrine, and then the village proper with a crooked street running down it. The chowkey seemed to know where to go. I pointed to the single buildings and he said, "Nay, sahib," and pointed to the street. So I posted a man to picket the shrine and led the rest through the bush behind our scruffy guide. He moved like a beaten dog, crouching and limping, bare-foot. There was a dead ox in the bush and a pair of kites sleeping and gorged beside it. It stank like a bad death. Turned me. We hurried on. The bushes were in flower, sort of wisteria, the blossoms closed and drooping. We crept along under a tumble-down wall and paused, kneeling, at the street corner. I posted two men there, one on each side with fixed bayonets, to fire down the street if he bolted. The other two sections would be covering it from the other end. Then I nudged the chowkey man and signalled to my grenade man and rifleman to cover me in. I slipped round the corner and went gingerly down the street. Suddenly I feel quite cool and excited at the same time. The chowkey went about fifteen yards down the street and then slunk against the wall on his knees, pointing inwards to the house he was kneeling against. It was made of branches woven with straw and reed, a beggared place. He looked up at me and my revolver and he was sweating with fear. I took a breath to steady myself, took the first pressure on my trigger, kicked the door lattice aside and jumped in. Stand in the light in the doorway and you're a dead man.

I crouched in the dark corner. It was very dark in there still. There was a pile of straw on the floor and straw heaped in the corner. And some huge thing moved ponderously. I nearly yelped. Then I saw what it was. It was a cow. Honestly. A sleepy fawn cow with a soft mild face like somebody's dream woman.

"She never frew no bomb," Chalky said. He was my rifleman. Cool as ice. His voice must have broken the fellow's nerve. There was a huge rustle in the straw in the corner behind the cow and a man stood up, a man in a white dhoti, young, thin, sort of smiling. Discoloured teeth. Chalky lunged his bayonet. The chap still had plenty of nerve left. He just swayed a little.

"Please," he said. "Have you got a smoke upon you?"

"Watch him, White," I said. I searched him.

"Please," he said. "I have nothing." He was breathing quickly and smiling.

"Come on," I said. "Quietly."

"You know you are taking me to my death?" he said. "No doubt?"

"I'm taking you to Poona," I said. "You killed three of our men."

The smile sort of congealed on his face. Like a trick. His head nodded like an old doll. "Did I?" he said. "Three men died? Did I?"

"Come on," I said. "It's daylight."

"It's dreadful," he said. He looked sick. I felt sorry for him, nodding his head and sick, sallow. Looked like a student, I should say.

"Keep your hands up," Chalky said, prodding him in the back.

We went quietly down the street, no incident at all, and I signalled the two enveloping sections together and we got down the road out of sight. I was in a cold sweat and I wanted to laugh.

The trucks weren't there. God, I cursed them, waiting there.

They might bitch the whole show. The villagers were going to the well quite close.

"What did you do it for, mate?" I heard Bottomley ask.

After a long silence the chap said very quietly, "For my country."

Chalky said, "Everybody says that. Beats me." Then we heard the trucks, and Chalky said, "We ought to be there in time for breakfast, boys."

# Questions for Discussion and Suggestions for Writing

(Suggestions for writing are marked with an asterisk)

## At All Costs

1  What do you learn about the ordinary routine of trench warfare from this story?

2  What impression do you gain of Captain Hanley from his behaviour,
   (a) before
   (b) after he hears the news of the forthcoming attack and the part his company is expected to play? Do you think he is a good company commander? Explain why.

3  Study the scene in which the Colonel breaks the news of the attack and gives the orders to the officers. How do (a) the Colonel, (b) the other officers feel during this scene? What is the significance of the line: "Hanley noticed how clean the colonel's gas bag was."

4  Why does Williams volunteer? What do you think of his reasons for doing so?

5  The men "only knew they were 'in for a show'". Why did the officers not tell them any more than that they must hold their positions "at all costs". Should they have told the men more? Give your reasons.

6  What do you consider to be Richard Aldington's aim in *At All Costs?* Discuss how the story is constructed in order to achieve that aim and comment on those parts which you found most effective.

*7  Write the diary entry that one of the subalterns might have made on the night before the attack.

## It's Just The Way It Is

8  What details of the setting in which the events take place does H.E.Bates include? Why are they included?

9  Why have the man and woman come to visit the Wing Commander? Discuss how they behave during their visit. Does the visit help them in any way?

10 What is your impression of the Wing Commander? What are his feelings as he watches the man and woman walk away? Could he have said or done anything more than he did?

*11 Write a poem or a song lyric entitled "That's War".

## A Horseman in the Sky

12 What background information about Carter Druse does the author include to enable us to judge what kind of a soldier he is before the main incidents of the story occur?

13 Discuss the awful decision that Carter Druse had to make. Why did he decide to fire? At the end of the story do you admire, despise or pity him?

*14 Write your own story about a soldier; call it "The Decision". Make it clear to the reader exactly why your main character makes up his mind to act as he does.

## The Drummer Boy of Shiloh

15 What is the boy thinking and feeling as he lies awake alone the night before the battle?

16 Discuss what the general says to the boy and why he says it. What is your impression of the general?

17 What effect do the general's words have on the boy? Why does he move the drum after the general has gone?

18 Why does Ray Bradbury set the story in a peach orchard?

*19 Write your own story called "The Night Before the Battle".

## Looking For Annie

20 Why did the narrator join the navy? What sort of person does he reveal himself to be in this story and what is his attitude towards himself?

21 What are the main features of Annie's character? Why did he and the narrator become friends?

22 Why did the narrator decide to go to visit Annie and what happened when he did? Discuss how the ending is constructed in order to create suspense and surprise.

*23 Write a story or poem entitled "Reported Missing".

## A Mystery of Heroism

24 Why does Fred Collins set out for the well? Should the colonel have forbidden him to go?

25 What are Collins's thoughts and feelings as he is on the way across the field to the well? How do they change while he is drawing the water?

26 What are his feelings as he dashes back across the field? Why does he at first go past the dying man and then return to him?

27 What is the significance of the ending? What do you think Stephen Crane wants the reader to learn about heroes and heroism from reading this story?

*28 Write a poem or a story with the title "The Hero".

## Beware of the Dog

29 What sort of a man is the pilot? What qualities of his character are revealed, (a) by his behaviour before he bails out, (b) by his behaviour in the hospital?

30 What is the significance of the fly which the pilot sees on the ceiling?

31 Discuss how Roald Dahl supplies the reader with evidence to suggest that everything is not as it should be at the hospital, in order to create suspense.

32 There are two tense incidents at the end of the story. Which of them is the climax? Explain why.

*33 Write a story about a pilot shot down in enemy occupied territory, who is found by some inhabitants of the occupied country. Describe the conversation in which they discuss what to do with him.

## Shall Not Perish

34 Why does the boy's mother go to visit Major de Spain? What does he say to her about why his son died? How and why is she able to help him?

35 How do the visit to Major de Spain's and his recollections of his grandfather's behaviour at the pictures help the boy to understand what his brother died for?

36 Discuss how the title *Shall Not Perish* summarises the message Faulkner is putting across in this story.

*37 Write a story or a poem called "The Telegram".

## Christmas Truce

38 Why did young Stan call on his grandad? What arguments does he use to try to persuade his grandad? What is your opinion of his arguments? Can you suggest other arguments he might have used that would have presented his case better?

39 What happened during the two Christmas truces? In what ways was the second Christmas truce different from the first?

40 Why does his grandfather want Stan to hear the story of the Christmas truces? What argument does he put forward based on the evidence of what happened during the truces? What is your opinion of his argument?

41 "Stan personifies the idealism of youth, while his grandad represents the wisdom of experience and age." Discuss this comment in the light of Dodger's final remarks to Stan.

*42 Write a newspaper article entitled "Why I am in favour of nuclear disarmament" or "Why I believe nuclear arms help to keep the peace".


## The Non-Combatant

43 Why was Cockerell usually appointed as billeting officer? Discuss how he dealt with the people of St Grégoire and explain why he tore up the note and wrote another one.

44 Why were the battalion recalled before they could get any rest and how did they react to the order to return? How did Cockerell and the remains of his platoon feel after the action while they were on their way to the rendezvous?

45 Explain exactly what happened to Cockerell and his men the night after they had retaken the Redoubt. Why did Cockerell feel a fool when he got back to St Grégoire? What is your final impression of him?

46 Why is the story called *The Non-combatant?* What did you learn from it about what life was like in the infantry during the First World War?

*47 Retell the story about the billet, the note and the major as Cockerell might have told it to some friends. You can either imagine you are Cockerell or write it as a playscript.


## Going Home

48 How do the room and the other people around him affect

Will as he lies waiting to be treated? What makes him tense and what helps him to relax?

49 When the doctor tells Will that he can go back to his unit why is Will unable to tell him his thoughts? Would it have helped him if he had spoken to the doctor?

50 Why is Will so depressed at the thought of going back to the war? What is your final impression of him?

*51 Write a story about a soldier who is wounded and invalided home.

## The Raid

52 Discuss the character of the Colonel. What features of his character are revealed by the way he talks to Selden?

53 What is Selden's attitude towards the job he is given to do? How and why does it change as he carries out the orders he has been given? What is your final impression of Selden?

54 What is your impression of the Indian who threw the bomb? Do you think the author intends us to feel any sympathy for him? Explain why.

*55 Write the official report that Selden might have written describing the raid or write a story called "The Raid".

## General

*56 Choose any two stories and explain what you learned from them about the way war affects people.

*57 Compare the view of war that is given in these stories with the view that is given in war films and war comics.

# The Authors

### Richard Aldington

Born in 1892 and educated at Dover College and London University. He served on the Western Front during the First World War and was badly gassed. After the war he worked as a writer, poet and translator, making his name with the bitter war book, *Death of a Hero*. He died in 1962.

### H. E. Bates

Educated at Kettering Grammar School, H.E. Bates (1905–74) published his first book at the age of twenty. Over the next fifteen years he established a reputation as a writer with his stories about life in the English countryside. In the Second World War he was commissioned into the RAF to write short stories, which would provide the general public with insights into the real dramas of wartime flying and into the lives of the pilots and their crews. The two collections of stories that he wrote – *The Greatest People in the World*, which included "It's Just The Way It Is", and *How Sleep The Brave* – were published under the pseudonym of Flying Officer X. He eventually reached the rank of Squadron Leader and the visits he paid to Burma and India, while in the RAF, provided him with the background that he used in his novels *The Purple Plain*, *The Jacaranda Tree* and *The Scarlet Sword*. His novel, *Fair Stood the Wind for France* (1944), about the experiences of the crew of a Wellington bomber which crashes in German-occupied France on its way home from a mission to Italy, is included in the Longman Imprint series. He was an extraordinarily prolific writer and wrote over 600 short stories. A selection, chosen by Geoffrey Halson, entitled *The Good Corn and other stories*, is also included in the Imprint series.

### Ambrose Bierce

Born in Ohio in 1842 Ambrose Bierce joined the army and fought in the American Civil War of 1861–65. He was commissioned on the field of battle and reached the rank of captain. After the war he became a journalist and at the age of twenty-six was appointed editor of the San Francisco *Newsletter and California Advertiser*. He became known as a master of invective and his swingeing articles made him many enemies. In 1887 he was· approached by the newspaper magnate William Randolph Hearst and subsequently for more than twenty years worked chiefly as a gossip columnist on Hearst's newspapers. In later life he became increasingly drunken and eccentric, quarrelling with almost all his relations and friends and finally with Hearst. In 1913, at the age of seventy-one, he disappeared while on a visit to Mexico. He wrote a considerable number of short stories, many of them on macabre themes, and was a keen collector of supernatural stories. There are few collections of his stories currently available, but a number of them can be found in an edition of the stories of Edgar Allan Poe and Ambrose Bierce in the Pegasus Library series (Harrap).

### Ray Bradbury

One of the best-known American writers of science fiction. Born in Illinois in 1920 he began, like many other science fiction writers, by contributing stories to magazines. In 1947 he wrote the screenplay for the film of *Moby Dick* and in 1953 he won the Benjamin Franklin Award for the best American magazine story. His collections of short stories, which are widely enjoyed by student readers, include *The Illustrated Man, The Golden Apples of the Sun* and *The Machineries of Joy*, all published in paperback by Corgi. His full-length novels, such as *The Silver Locusts* and *Fahrenheit 451*, both available in Corgi editions, are also popular.

### Charles Causley

One of Britain's leading poets. Born in 1917 in the Cornish town of Launceston, he first started writing poetry while he was serving in the Royal Navy during the Second World War. Of his wartime experiences he has written: "What affected me as much as anything during those wartime years was the fact that the companion who left with me for the Navy on that same day was later drowned in a convoy to northern Russia. From that moment, I found myself haunted by the words in the twenty-fourth chapter of St Matthew: 'Then shall two be in the field; the one shall be taken, and the other left.'"

## Stephen Crane

Born in Newark, New Jersey in 1871, Stephen Crane died at the edge of twenty-nine in 1900. He worked as a journalist and was a war correspondent in Cuba and in Greece. Many of his stories dealt with the violence he experienced in the life around him. He is best known for his war novel, *The Red Badge of Courage*, which was published in 1895.

## Roald Dahl

Born in South Wales in 1916 to Norwegian parents, Roald Dahl went to Repton School. He took part in an expedition exploring the interior of Newfoundland, then joined the Shell Oil Company. In 1939, when the Second World War broke out, he joined the R.A.F. He served as a fighter pilot in Libya, Greece and Spain, before being posted to Washington in 1942 as Assistant Air Attaché. While there he began to write and his first collection of stories, *Over To You*, in which *Beware of the Dog*, was included, was published in 1944. At the end of the war he was working in Intelligence and had been promoted to the rank of Wing Commander. Roald Dahl is well-known as a writer of mystery and suspense short stories and his collections *Kiss, Kiss* (Penguin) and *Someone Like You* (Penguin) have been translated into many languages. He is one of Britain's leading children's book authors. His books for children include *The Magic Finger*, *Charlie and the Chocolate Factory* and *Danny, The Champion of the World*.

## William Faulkner

Born in Ripley, Mississippi in 1897, he worked for a while in a bank, before going to the University of Mississippi. During the First World War he served in the Royal Air Force as a lieutenant. Afterwards he returned to Mississippi and took various jobs as a painter, paper-hanger and carpenter. Later, he worked on ships and did newspaper work in New Orleans, where he wrote his first novel, *Soldier's Pay*, published in 1926. He wrote his famous novel *As I Lay Dying*, published in 1930, between midnight and 4 a.m. while working as a coal-heaver. His other books include *The Sound and The Fury, Sanctuary* and *Go Down Moses*. In 1949 he was awarded the Nobel Prize for Literature.

## Robert Graves

Poet, novelist and short story writer, Robert Graves was born in 1895 and educated at Charterhouse School. He left school in 1914 and planned to go to Oxford University, but when the First World War broke out in that year he joined the army and did not go up to Oxford until 1919. He finally took his degree in 1926 and spent a year as Professor of English Literature at Cairo University before becoming a full-time writer. He has published over 120 books. His *Selected Poems* are included in the Penguin Poets series and in 1961 he was elected Professor of Poetry at Oxford University. He is widely known for his historical novels, such as *I, Claudius* which was successfully adapted for television. His autobiography, *Goodbye To All That,* published in 1929, in which he describes his experience of life in the trenches, is an established classic.

## Ian Hay

Ian Hay was the pseudonym of Major-General John Hay Beith, CBE, MC. Born in 1876 he was educated at Fettes School and St John's College, Cambridge. He became a schoolmaster and in 1907 published his first novel, *Pip.* He fought in the First World War and in 1915 his war epic, *The First Hundred Thousand,* was published. It was written while he was in France and posted home piecemeal whenever there was a post, so that it could first be serialised in Blackwood's Magazine. Subsequently he concentrated mainly on playwriting. He died in 1952.

## James S. Kenary

Born in Worcester, Massachusetts, USA, James S. Kenary spent four years in the Marine Corps, before going to the University of Massachusetts. "Going Home", which was included in the *Best American Short Stories of 1973,* was his first published short story.

## Alun Lewis

Born in Aberdare in 1915, Alun Lewis was educated at Cowbridge Grammar School and the University College of Wales,

Aberystwyth. He joined the army during the Second World War and in 1943 was posted to India. In 1944 he was killed in an accident in Burma. A poet and short story writer, he has been described as one of the two best poets produced by the war.

# Further Reading

ARNOTHY, CHRISTINE. *I am Fifteen and I Do Not Want to Die,* Fontana.

BATES, H.E. *The Greatest People in the World,* Cape.

BATES, H.E. *Fair Stood the Wind for France,* Longman Imprint Books.

BOULLE, P. *The Bridge on the River Kwai,* Heinemann New Windmill.

BRADDON, RUSSELL. *The Naked Island,* Evans.

BRICKHILL, PAUL. *Reach for the Sky,* Collins.

BRICKHILL, PAUL. *The Dambusters,* Pan.

BRICKHILL, PAUL. *Escape or Die,* Pan.

BRUCE, GEORGE, ed. *Short Stories of the First World War,* Sidgwick and Jackson.

CHAMBERS, AIDAN ed. *Fighters in the Sky,* Macmillan Topliners.

CHAMBERS, AIDAN, ed. *Men at War,* Macmillan Topliners.

CRANE, STEPHEN. *The Red Badge of Courage,* Nelson.

FORESTER, C.S. *The Gun,* Longman.

FRANK, ANNE. *The Diary of Anne Frank,* Pan.

GALLICO, PAUL. *The Snow Goose,* Penguin.

GIBSON, GUY. *Enemy Coast Ahead,* Pan.

GRAVES, ROBERT. *Goodbye To All That,* Penguin.

GREENE, GRAHAM. *The Quiet American,* Penguin.

HAY, IAN. *The First Hundred Thousand,* Corgi.

HARRIS, JOHN. *The Professionals,* Puffin.

HAUTZIG, ESTHER. *The Endless Steppe,* Heinemann New Windmill, Peacock.

HELLER, JOSEPH. *Catch 22,* Corgi.

HEMINGWAY, ERNEST. *A Farewell To Arms,* Penguin.

HEMINGWAY, ERNEST. *For Whom The Bell Tolls,* Penguin.

HERSEY, JOHN. *Hiroshima,* Penguin.

HILLARY, RICHARD. *The Last Enemy,* Macmillan, Pan.

HOLBROOK, DAVID. *Fleshwounds,* Longman Imprint Books.

HUNT, IRENE. *Across Five Aprils,* Heinemann New Windmill.
JOHNSON, B.S. ed. *The Evacuees,* Gollancz.
MACLEAN, ALISTAIR. *The Guns of Navarone,* Fontana.
MAILER, NORMAN. *The Naked and the Dead,* Panther.
MARLAND, MICHAEL and WILLCOX, ROBIN, ed. *While They Fought,* Longman Imprint Books.
MARSH, WILLIAM. *Company K* (abridged by Dennis Pepper), Nelson Getaway.
MINCO, MARGA. *Bitter Herbs,* Wheaton.
ORWELL, GEORGE. *Homage To Catalonia,* Penguin.
PEPPER, DENNIS, ed. *A Time To Fight,* Nelson Getaway.
PHILLIPS, C.E. LUCAS. *Cockleshell Heroes,* Pan.
RAWICZ, SLAVOMIR. *The Long Walk,* Pan.
REID, P.R. *The Colditz Story,* Hodder.
REMARQUE, ERICH MARIA. *All Quiet On the Western Front,* Heinemann New Windmill.
RICHARDS, FRANK. *Old Soldiers Never Die,* Faber.
SASSOON, SIEGFRIED. *Memoirs of An Infantry Officer,* Faber.
SHAW, ROBERT. *The Hiding Place,* Penguin.
SHERRY, SYLVIA. *Dark River, Dark Mountain,* Heinemann New Windmill.
SHUTE, NEVIL. *A Town Like Alice,* Heinemann New Windmill.
SHUTE, NEVIL. *Pied Piper,* Heinemann New Windmill.
SOUTHALL, IVAN. *Seventeen Seconds,* Brockhampton.
STEINBECK, JOHN. *The Moon is Down,* Heinemann New Windmill.
WALSH, JILL PATON. *Fireweed,* Puffin.
WALSH, JILL PATON. *The Dolphin Crossing,* Puffin.
WESTALL, ROBERT. *The Machine Gunners,* Puffin.
WILLIAMS, ERIC. *The Wooden Horse,* Fontana.
WOODFORD, PEGGY. *Backwater War,* Bodley Head.

## Plays

ARDEN, JOHN. *Sergeant Musgrave's Dance,* Methuen.
HALL, WILLIS. *The Long and the Short and the Tall,* Heinemann Hereford Plays.
MCGRATH, JOHN. *Events While Guarding a Bofors Gun,* Methuen Playscripts.
MANVELL, ROGER. *The July Plot,* Blackie Student Drama.
SHERRIFF, R.C. *Journey's End,* Heinemann Hereford Plays.
WESKER, ARNOLD. *Chips With Everything,* Blackie Student Drama.
WHITING, JOHN. *Marching Song,* Heinemann Hereford Plays.

## Poetry

GARDNER, BRIAN. *Up the Line to Death*, Methuen.
GARDNER, BRIAN. *The Terrible Rain*, Methuen.
HAMILTON, I. *The Poetry of War*, 1939–45, Allen Ross.
OWEN, WILFRED. *Poems*, Chatto and Windus.
PARSONS, I. *Men Who March Away*, Chatto and Windus.

# Films

*All Quiet on the Western Front* (Based on the novel by Erich Maria Remarque, it tells the story of a group of German teenage boys who volunteer to fight in the war, fired by the patriotic enthusiam of their school teacher.) 103 minutes, MCA Films.

*The Long and the Short and the Tall* (Based on the play by Willis Hall.) 105 minutes, Warner.

*The Red Badge of Courage* (Based on the novel by Stephen Crane.) 69 minutes, Ron Harris.

*Incident At Owl Creek* (Based on the short story, An Occurrence At Owl Creek Bridge by Ambrose Bierce.) 27 minutes, Connoisseur.

*The War Game* (Made for BBC television, but never shown because it was considered to be too horrifying. An examination of what the effect of nuclear war would be on both individuals and society as a whole.) 47 minutes, B.F.I.

*Culloden* (A documentary reconstruction of the Battle of Culloden, made by Peter Watkins, who also directed *The War Game*. The documentary style of the film, which was made for television, brings out the real horror of war.) 70 minutes, Concord.

*Children of the Ashes* (The story of Hiroshima.) 40 minutes, Concord.

*Children of Hiroshima* (An extract from a Japanese film depicting the dropping of the bomb.) 10 minutes, Contemporary.

*A Plague on Your Children* (An account of research into chemical and biological methods of warfare in Britain.) 70 minutes, Concord.

## Addresses of film distributors

British Film Institute (Distribution Department), 42–3 Lower Marsh, London SE1

Concord Films Council, Nacton, Ipswich, Suffolk.

Connoisseur Films Ltd., 167 Oxford Street, London W1.

Contemporary Films Ltd., 55 Greek Street, London W1V 6DB

MCA Films, Kingston Road, Merton Park, London SW 19.

Ron Harris Cinema Services Ltd., Glenbuck House, Glenbuck Road, Surbiton, Surrey.

Warner-Pathé Distribution Ltd., Warner-Pathé House, 135 Wardour Street, London W1.

**Longman Imprint Books**
*General Editor* Michael Marland

Titles in the Series
**There is a Happy Land** Keith Waterhouse
**Nine African Stories** Doris Lessing
**The Experience of Colour** *edited by* Michael Marland
**The Human Element and other stories** Stan Barstow
**The Leaping Lad and other stories** Sid Chaplin
**Z Cars** Four television scripts
**Steptoe and Son** Four television scripts
**Conflicting Generations** Five television scripts
**A Sillitoe Selection** Alan Sillitoe
**Late Night on Watling Street and other stories** Bill Naughton
**Black Boy** Richard Wright
**The Millstone** Margaret Drabble
**Fair Stood the Wind for France** H. E. Bates
**Scene Scripts** Seven television plays
**The Experience of Work** *edited by* Michael Marland
**Breaking Away** *edited by* Marilyn Davies *and* Michael Marland
**The Kraken Wakes** John Wyndham
**A Hemingway Selection** Ernest Hemingway
**Friends and Families** *edited by* Eileen *and* Michael Marland
**Ten Western Stories** *edited by* C.E.J. Smith
**The Good Corn and other stories** H.E. Bates
**The Experience of Sport** *edited by* John L. Foster
**Loves, Hopes, and Fears** *edited by* Michael Marland
**The African Queen** C.S. Forester
**A Casual Acquaintance and other stories** Stan Barstow
**Eight American Stories** *edited by* D.L. James
**Cider with Rosie** Laurie Lee
**The L-Shaped Room** Lynne Reid Banks
**Softly, Softly** Five television scripts by Elwyn Jones
**The Pressures of life** Four television plays
**The Experience of Prison** *edited by* David Ball
**Saturday Night and Sunday Morning** Alan Sillitoe
**A John Wain Selection** John Wain
**Jack Schaefer and the American West** Jack Schaefer
**Goalkeepers are Crazy** Brain Glanville
**A James Joyce Selection** James Joyce
**Out of the Air** Five radio plays, *edited by* Alfred Bradley
**Could it be?** *edited by* Michael Marland
**The Minority Experience** *edited by* Michael Marland *and* Sarah Ray
**Scene Scripts Two** Five television plays
**Caribbean Stories** *edited by* Michael Marland
**An Isherwood Selection** *edited by* Geoffrey Halson
**A Thomas Hardy Selection** *edited by* Geoffrey Halson
**While They Fought** *edited by* Michael Marland *and* Robin Willcox
**The Wave and other stories** Liam O'Flaherty
**Irish Short Stories** *edited by* Frances Crowe
**The Experience of Parenthood** *edited by* Chris Buckton

**The Birds and other stories**  Daphne du Maurier
**A D.H. Lawrence Selection**  *edited by* Geoffrey Halson
**Twelve War Stories**  *edited by* John L. Foster
**The Experience of Love**  *edited by* Michael Marland

Companion cassettes, with readings of some of the key stories are
available for the following:
**The Leaping Lad and other stories**
**The Human Element**
**A Sillitoe Selection**
**Late Night on Watling Street**
**A Casual Acquaintance**
**Loves, Hopes, and Fears**
**A John Wain Selection**

# Acknowledgements

We are grateful to the following for permission to reproduce copyright material:

The author's agent for the story "At All Costs" by Richard Aldington from *Short Stories of the First World War* edited by George Bruce, © Catherine Guillaume; George Allen & Unwin (Publishers) Ltd. for the story "The Raid" by Alun Lewis from *In The Green Tree*; the author's agent and the Estate of the late H.E. Bates for the story "It's Just the Way It Is" by H.E. Bates from *The Stories of Flying Officer "X"* published by Jonathan Cape Ltd.; the author's agent for the story "The Drummer Boy of Shiloh" by Ray Bradbury from *The Saturday Evening Post Stories* Volume 7. Reprinted by permission of A.D. Peters & Co. Ltd.; the author's agent for the story "Looking for Annie" by Charles Causley from *Hand to Dance and Skylark* published by Robson Books; the author's agent for the story "Beware of the Dog" by Roald Dahl from *Over To You* published by Penguin Books Ltd., © Roald Dahl 1945; the author's agent for the story "Shall Not Perish" by William Faulkner from *Uncle Willy and Other Stories*; the author's agent for the story "Christmas Truce" from *Collected Stories* by Robert Graves, © Robert Graves 1965; the author's agent for the story "The Non-Combatant" by Ian Hay from *Carrying On – After The First Hundred Thousand* published by Samuel French Ltd.; The Massachusetts Review for the story "Going Home" by James S. Kenary in *The Massachusetts Review* Volume XIII, No. 4, © 1972 The Massachusetts Review, Inc.

"A Mystery of Heroism" by Stephen Crane is from *Stephen Crane: An Omnibus* by Stephen Crane, by permission of Alfred A. Knopf. Inc.

We are grateful to the following for permission to reproduce
photographs:
Cooper-Hewitt Museum, New York, the Smithsonian Institu-
tion's national museum of design, pages 25, 33 and 49; John
Hillelson Agency, page 67 (photo: Constantine Manos) and
cover (photo: Don McCullin); Imperial War Museum, London
pages 1, 55, 79, 97 and 135; Popperfoto, page 19; Studio St Ives,
St Ives, Cornwall, page 39; Time Inc 1973, page 119 (photo:
M Rougier/LIFE).